TO CATCH
A BRIDE

TO CATCH
A BRIDE

BY

RENEE ROSZEL

MILLS & BOON®

To Dr Rebecca Sims,
a woman with brains, beauty, grace and kindness.
Welcome to the family, Becky!

*First published in Great Britain 2001
Large Print edition 2001
Harlequin Mills & Boon Limited,
Eton House, 18-24 Paradise Road,
Richmond, Surrey TW9 1SR*

© Renee Roszel Wilson 2001

ISBN 0 263 17250 3

*Set in Times Roman 16½ on 18 pt.
16-1101-48984*

*Printed and bound in Great Britain
by Antony Rowe Ltd, Chippenham, Wiltshire*

CHAPTER ONE

KALLI dashed into Nikolos Varos's private office, consumed with grief and unreasoning panic. Thankfully, no watchdog of a secretary sat at the reception desk to run interference. Kalli couldn't cope with making explanations. She needed to get this done and done quickly—hopefully without hysterics.

Her mental turmoil kept her from taking notice of the immense high-rise office. She already knew Mr. Varos was vastly prosperous, but in her emotional state the physical trappings held no interest for her. Working hard to hold back tears, she headed toward a tall, gaunt man standing behind a gleaming desk of stainless steel and glass. She planted both hands on the cool, orderly desktop and focused on his striped tie, too grief-stricken and ashamed to look at his face.

Coward! she shouted inwardly. *Look him in the eye! Anybody who jilts her fiancé on their wedding day should do it face-to-face, not sniveling at the floor like a mouse!*

Sick to her stomach, she lifted her gaze. Her heart pounded so deafeningly, she wasn't sure she would be able to hear her words when she spoke them.

"Mr. Varos," she began, amazed that her voice rang with conviction. "I can't go through with the wedding."

The man's eyes widened and he opened his mouth to speak, but she forged on, giving him no opening. "My grandfather passed away during the night. When Mother called to tell me, I realized I'd agreed to this marriage for him—because I love—*loved* him. This arrangement was something *he* wanted. It wasn't what I wanted at all. I went along—out of family loyalty."

He opened his mouth again, but she threw up her hand to halt him. "I know, I know—my family's Greek and very traditional and so is yours. And yes, my mother's arranged marriage was a good one. And, it's true that our grandfathers were lifelong friends and their fondest wish was to join our two families." She grasped desperately for the right words—

anything that didn't sound lame. "But, I'm an American, Mr. Varos. I was born in the United States and I—I can't do this! Please understand and—and one day try to forgive me."

Spinning on her heel, she fled, calling herself the chicken-hearted baby she was. Running away was unforgivable, but she was too close to hysteria and emotional collapse to deal with ranting and raving, no matter how much she deserved it.

She told herself this was for the best. After all, the marriage was little more than a business deal, certainly not a love match. To make that painfully obvious, where had she finally found her so-called fiancé? In his office! At seven o'clock in the morning on his wedding day!

Besides, she hadn't even met the man. His international finance dealings had kept him out of the country until the last minute. Considering all that, how important could the wedding—or *she*—be to him?

Surely he'd had deals fall through before. He'd be disappointed, maybe even annoyed, but he'd get over it. When she was more herself, when her grief had ebbed, she vowed to write a letter of apology.

She felt so alone. Oh, if only Grandpa Chris hadn't taken a drastic turn for the worse just as she and her mother, Zoe, were about to leave for California. Zoe Angelis had cared for her father-in-law for so many years, she'd felt compelled to stay behind with the dear man as his health failed and miss her only child's wedding. Kalli knew Zoe had been torn, but being the kind of woman she was, Zoe couldn't leave Grandpa Chris to depart this world alone. Kalli understood, of course, and wouldn't have had it any other way, but right now she felt desolate, lost, and needed her mother's unwavering support.

Now that the wedding was off, all she had to do was get back to her hotel, pack her bags and fly out of San Francisco. She must get back to Kansas to be with her mother and say her last goodbyes to Grandpa Chris.

The first day of June was turning into a nightmare for Nikolos Varos. His flight from Tokyo had been delayed, not once but twice, making him almost miss his own wedding. Then, in the wee hours, when he'd arrived at his pent-house apartment, he discovered a plumbing leak. The place was a disaster, so he'd had to dress for the formal wedding breakfast in his office bathroom.

And now, as he slipped on his tux jacket, the fiancée he had yet to meet came running into his office announcing to his bewildered assistant that she couldn't marry him.

Peering around the corner where his executive dressing room adjoined his office, he scanned the space, empty now, except for his buttoned-up, button-down administrative assistant. The poor guy stood as though frozen, staring toward the office's exit.

Niko leaned against the doorjamb and heaved a weary exhale. "What's the matter, Charles?" he queried, cynicism ripe in his tone. "Never been jilted?"

Niko's sarcasm seemed to bring his assistant out of his stupor and he turned, his long, thin face ashen. "Is that what happened, sir?"

Niko shook his head, feeling out of kilter from jet lag and lack of sleep. He'd hardly closed his eyes in the last seventy-two hours, getting his schedule squared away for an extended honeymoon, and now this? "I'm new at being dumped, but that little speech sounded like 'goodbye' to me."

He scanned Charles, meticulously groomed, a fastidious detail-man with a prominent patrician nose and the pallor of desk work. Even as naturally pale and grave as he was, Charles looked so bleak Niko almost felt sorry for him.

For him?

Niko sensed the full impact of what just occurred hadn't hit him yet. He was too tired to be furious. But he had a feeling it would register any minute.

Pushing away from the wall, he adjusted his tuxedo jacket. "No point standing around licking my wounds. There are things to be done."

"Shall I inform the guests, sir?"

"What?" Niko frowned, surprised by the question. "Of course not."

"But, sir—"

"Charles," he cut in, not planning to discuss whose job it was to inform *his* friends that *his* wedding had been canceled by *his* fiancée. "While I'm giving the bad news to my guests, get that woman's phone number."

"You want me to call your fiancée at her hotel?" He sounded worried.

Niko reached the doors to his office and turned back. His brain was starting to record the significance of what happened, and his gut began to burn. *He'd been discarded like an old pair of shoes, on his wedding day. People had come from all over the world to attend the festivities. Royalty, political heads of state, even a smattering of Hollywood glitterati. Five hundred guests cooled their heels in a ballroom fifty floors below, while his personal future and his pride were being kicked in the teeth by a wisp of a woman from Kansas—of all places! And now, here he stood, looking like a blasted head waiter who'd just lost his job!*

"Damn straight I want you to call my fiancée at her hotel." He turned to go, then stopped to look back. "Rather my ex-fiancée."

"What do you want me to say, sir?"

"Don't worry, Charles. I'll tell you what to say when I return." He stalked out the door. His head pounded as his travel-weary brain finally grasped the ugly extent of his predicament—humiliation on a global scale. He jabbed the elevator button to take him down to where the stately breakfast was about to begin. In mere moments he would face the most humbling, emasculating situation he could imagine. In a very public, very costly venue, he would be compelled to admit that, on the threshold of their wedding, his bride-to-be discovered she couldn't bring herself to marry him.

He stared at the elevator door, wondering if he punched it whether his fist would leave its impression. He shook his head, running an agitated hand through his hair. It would be stupid to break his knuckles simply because some little Kansas hayseed got cold feet. He jabbed the elevator button again, a rush of self-contempt washing over him.

He—Nikolos Varos—who'd always been so condescending of his friends' broken marriages, scornful of how they hadn't been able to keep their families together. Nothing like that would happen to him, he'd thought. He was superior, above the fray. Even his parents hadn't been able to hold their love match together. But *he* would. *He* could. "But look at you," he grumbled, "Mr. Above-The-Fray can't even get a countrified bumpkin to walk down the aisle."

After years of listening to his parents arguments, and hearing his friends whimper, brokenhearted over women, he'd decided the old ways were better—to marry based on logic, common values and beliefs.

His brain taunted him with echoes of Kalli's blunt, hurried rejection and he gritted his teeth. His grandfather, Dionysus, had blathered on about the Angelis family for what seemed like forever. About how, at the age of twelve, Dion had saved Christos Angelis from drowning in a fishing accident. They'd been best friends ever since, and had vowed to join the two families. At first the idea of marrying some stranger from Kansas had only made Niko laugh, but he'd been handed her picture and found her appealing—at least, physically.

Though she wasn't a classic beauty, she had a lot of dark, shiny hair, large, lavender eyes and a strangely haunting smile. He had to admit, her picture was hardly a negative factor in his tally. Also on the plus side, the Varos family and the Angelis family came from the town of Kouteopothi, in Greece. They had common roots, held common beliefs, traditions. Most importantly, the families were bound by an all-

consuming longing between two elderly gentlemen to see an old promise kept.

It hadn't taken as much soul-searching as
Niko believed it would to warm to the pros-
pect. Being a man who put great stock in logic
and order, he finally bowed to his grandfather's coaxing.

Business had kept him away from the States,
and he'd had to put off, then ultimately cancel,
several planned meetings with Kalli. Still, that
didn't mean he hadn't grown accustomed to
the idea of marriage to her. He'd given her a
very fair settlement in their prenuptial agreement. Damn it, he'd even changed his will!

And little Miss Hayloft blithely skips into
his office on their wedding day and hacks his
well-ordered plans to shreds. His anger surged.
Not a man to make weak or empty threats, he
growled, ''Miss Kalli Angelis, you won't get
away with this.'' The elevator doors whooshed
open and he stepped inside.

''I won't need much time,'' he pledged, as
he formulated his vendetta. ''Three weeks will
do.''

The elevator doors slid shut and Nikolos
Varos began his descent.

*   *   *

Kalli didn't want to think about anything right now, not the look on her ex-fiancé's face when she told him she couldn't marry him, not the fact that she had a long, dreary day ahead of her, trying to get back to Kansas City. And she definitely didn't want to dwell on how best to pack one, unused wedding dress.

What was she going to do with it once she got it home, sell it? She and her mother had spent hours sewing hundreds of beads on the lace bodice and sleeves, beads from dozens of faux pearl necklaces they'd scrounged from garage sales. She peered at the white confection and experienced a self-condemning twinge. All that time and effort had been such a harebrained waste. An arranged marriage, for goodness' sake! Had she gone temporarily insane?

Expelling a resigned sigh, she rolled up the dress and shoved it into the suitcase.

Mashing down on the hastily deposited clothes, she struggled with the suitcase zipper. ''Do not feel sorry for yourself, Kalli Angelis!'' She sniffed. ''You weren't in love with the man. You'd only seen one old snapshot of him—when he was seventeen, yet!''

She had to admit the grown man in the office didn't look much like the picture her grandpa had carried around in his wallet all those years.

According to Grandpa Chris, Nikolos had visited family in Kouteopothi—or as she laughingly translated it, "Crooked Foot"—the summer before her grandfather came to live with Kalli and her mother, Zoe. "Maybe the smile made all the difference," she mumbled. He definitely did *not* smile this morning when she'd barged into his office.

He seemed so pale and stiff. Not the image her grandpa had given. He'd said Niko was athletic and fun-loving, always laughing. Maybe over the years the business of international finance had sucked the fun and spontaneity out of him.

"Besides," she gritted out, yanking on the suitcase zipper. "Just because Grandpa Chris raved about how wonderful he was doesn't mean he would have made a good match for me. Money and position aren't everything."

With a hearty jerk, she coerced the suitcase into zipping shut and hefted it off the bed. The phone rang, startling her so badly she dropped the bag on her foot.

"Ouch!" Making a pained face at the telephone, she wondered who would be calling. Her mother? Who else? "Except maybe Mr. Varos," she muttered, "deciding he needs to take a shot at me before I get out of town."

Limping to the phone, she promised herself if it was Mr. Varos bent on his verbal pound of flesh, she could hang up. Another spineless act, but right now she had her own traumas to deal with. His would have to wait.

"Hello," she said. "Mama?"

There was a pause, then, "No."

She knew immediately who the voice belonged to. The subdued monosyllable could only have been stated by the starched, bloodless man she'd so recently jilted. "Oh—Mr. Varos." She swallowed. "I—I really can't talk now. I have to catch my flight." That wasn't totally accurate. She had standby status. All flights that would eventually get her to Kansas City were full. But he didn't need to know that.

"This will only take a moment."

She closed her eyes and sank to the mattress. "Oh?" Her life flashed before her eyes. There could be nothing more ominous than the sound of a perfectly calm voice when you *know* you deserve reaming out. All that solid, well-thought out logic going into an argument would be hard to debate.

On the other hand, Mr. Varos would discover her half of the ''debate'' would consist of banging the receiver in his ear. She tensed, ready to slam it down. ''How may I help you?'' She cringed the instant the words were out of her mouth. *Why don't you just hand him a knife?* she scolded inwardly. *You all but prodded him into saying, ''You can take a nosedive off a cliff, thank you very much!''*

''Since you are by profession a Historical Reconstruction Consultant, I would appreciate it if you'd remain in California for three weeks, stay at the recently purchased Victorian estate that would have been your home—to use your expertise in making it a showplace. As you know, that refurbishing project was part of the marriage agreement.'' Kalli sat up, not believing what she was hearing. ''The mansion must be renovated for an important gathering in six months, so time is of the essence.''

She shook her head in disbelief. He was a cool customer. She'd expected almost anything but this. He talked like a hotel concierge, making her the offer without a speck of anger or the hint of ruffled feathers. Of course *business deals* weren't usually fraught with emotion. How silly of her to have worried that her last-minute rejection would offend him.

Ha! Mr. Ice-Water-For-Blood-Banker was *not* only not angry, he was offering her a plum assignment. One of the reasons she'd agreed to the marriage, besides her desire to please her grandfather, had been the fact that Mr. Varos was an influential man with high-level connections.

Time and again as the wedding day approached, she'd told herself Mr. Varos would gain the wife-slash-hostess and two offspring he'd stipulated, and she would get a huge boost for her professional life. Logic had been her watchword, since soft emotions were not a part of the equation. She had reasoned turning the Varos mansion into a showplace would make her career, with her work depicted in slick, respected magazines such as *Architectural Digest*. Why should he be the only one to get everything he wanted out of the marriage? If he could have a career and children, why couldn't she?

"Miss Angelis?"

His solemn voice snapped her out of her stunned musings. "Oh—yes. I'm here."

"What do you say?"

She couldn't imagine that he would even ask, so the idea of accepting had never entered her mind. It was too fantastic. Jilting a man, then an hour later, having that same man offer her a spectacular job. "But—that's very—are you sure?"

"As you stated, Miss Angelis, you only have a minute. May I have your answer?"

Kalli was torn. Even pausing to consider such an offer was a blatant indication she wasn't paddling with all her oars. She sucked in a trembly breath. Her conscience was killing her over breaking her marriage promise. The fact that he would request that she do the work on his home after her abrupt rejection was amazingly tolerant. Did she dare contemplate it? *Did she dare refuse?* How many Kansas City historical reconstruction consultants got a shot at being featured in *Architectural Digest?*

"Are you there?"

Fumbling with the phone, she jerked out of her stupor. "Oh—yes—I'm here." She had a thought and had to voice it. "It's kind of you to offer me the job, considering—everything. Actually, that's a concern—"

"If I'm there at all, Miss Angelis," he cut in, "it won't be to see you, and any visit will be brief."

How did he know that's what she'd been about to ask? Did he read minds? Besides being tolerant he was intuitive. "Well—" She could feel herself wavering, weakening. If breaking her word didn't bother him, then who was she to deny herself this chance? "Naturally I'll need to be in Kansas City for my grandfather's—" Her voice wavered and she cleared her throat. Her loss was still too new and raw.

"Naturally," he said. "I trust a week in Kansas should be sufficient. Notify me of your flight schedule. Someone will meet you at the airport."

The phone went dead. After several seconds of absorbing the dial tone, Kalli realized he'd hung up, evidently concluding the deal was made.

Her head swam and she felt dazed, but she supposed he was correct. She hadn't said no. Planning the refurbishing of the Varos mansion would be good for both of them, really. Doing the job for him would help ease her angst over jilting him, not to mention it would double his property's value. Besides, all that exacting work would keep her mind occupied, so she wouldn't dwell on the empty hole in her heart left by her grandfather's passing.

"Uh—okay," she mumbled belatedly, lowering the receiver to its cradle. "I'll see you in a week, Mr. Varos."

She slumped there, staring at nothing for a long time. This had been a terrible, emotion-battering wedding day, full of grief and guilt. She'd acted like a mealymouthed double-crosser. Never in her life had she behaved so badly, and she was thoroughly ashamed. It seemed to go against nature that she should be rewarded by the very person she'd wronged.

At least, in her mind, she'd wronged him. To hear Mr. Varos's voice, you'd think this was just another day in his life, filled with endless columns of credits and debits. To Nikolos Varos, being tossed over by Kalli Angelis was obviously nothing more than a huge yawn.

She shook herself and straightened. Right now she didn't have the mental strength to be either puzzled or shocked by his indifference. She pushed off the bed and grabbed her suitcase. It was time to go home, comfort her mother and bid her beloved grandfather good-bye.

Kalli hurried from the hotel room, fighting a niggling unease.

Niko tugged the knit shirt on over his head and caught sight of himself in his office's bathroom mirror. Now that he'd shucked the tux, he might be dressed more comfortably, but his expression didn't exhibit any emotional comfort. He was so irate he was surprised smoke didn't billow from his ears.

As he reentered his office Charles hung up his telephone and rose from his leather chair.

"When is she coming?"

Charles turned, his expression solemn. "Next week. I said someone would pick her up at the airport, as you instructed." His perusal dropped to the desk and he began to straighten papers, clearly agitated. "How did you know she would accept, sir?" he asked, with a quick peek.

Niko stretched his shoulders, working to ease the tension in his muscles. "Greed, Charles. Greed and pride." He ground his teeth. "You dangle the right bait and the fish will bite."

Charles gathered up several file folders and hugged them to his suit front. "She thought I was you, sir." The man turned stiffly to face his boss, his expression almost, but not quite, accusing. Niko mouthed a curse. Blast the tribulations of having a brutally scrupulous workforce. Even such a slight subterfuge, like not correcting an inaccurate assumption, grated on Charles's sense of propriety. "You won't do anything rash, sir?"

The man's cautioning tone sent a rush of bitter resentment through Niko but he held his temper. "Of course not. I intend to plan my revenge very carefully."

Though it didn't seem possible, Charles' pallor increased. "But—but, sir, you made the CEO of Megatronics cry. You can be—"

"Don't be ridiculous. He didn't cry. He had an eye infection," Niko snapped, his reserve corroding. "More to the point, the man was a fool. He wasted millions by breaking his word and not heeding my advice. I only made him see the error of his ways." More to himself than to Charles, he muttered, "Miss Angelis will merely get some hands-on experience about how I deal with those who break their word to me."

"Oh—dear..." A sparkle of sweat beaded on Charles's forehead. His expression was so transparently fearful Niko experienced a twinge of compassion. His assistant was an excellent manager, but anything that smacked of ruthlessness made him queasy.

Pressing a hand on Charles's shoulder, Niko squeezed. "Don't look so worried. I'm not going to eat the woman alive." He smiled, but it felt more like a baring of teeth. "I'm merely going to indulge my little ex with some—undivided attention."

Charles winced, alerting Niko to the fact that his reassuring squeeze had became painful. He removed his hand. "Don't you think she deserves a little discomfort?"

Charles's Adam's apple bobbed, but he didn't respond.

Niko would have appreciated a glimmer of empathy from his hired right arm, but he didn't require it. He scanned the man shielding himself with a batch of files and scowled. "Maybe your attitude would be different if it was *your* face splashed all over the San Francisco press instead of mine," he gritted out, "and *you* were the laughingstock."

CHAPTER TWO

KALLI stepped off the plane in San Francisco, a week later, with no idea what to expect. That morning she'd called Mr. Varos's office to let him know her schedule, but couldn't get past some female receptionist, who assured huskily that the message would be passed to the proper department. So Kalli had no choice but to leave the flight information with a stranger on the phone.

She still had niggling doubts about accepting this job, doubts she could not squelch. Would she be left stranded in the airport as some kind of sadistic joke? She still couldn't imagine Mr. Varos, or anyone else for that matter, really being as magnanimous as he'd seemed when he'd offered her the assignment.

She emerged from the long gangway, side-stepping fellow passengers who had come to abrupt halts to embrace friends and loved ones. Other plane-mates charged by her, cellular phones pasted to an ear as they dashed hell-bent down the cavernous corridor toward baggage claim, taxi cabs and business meetings.

The place was awash with humanity, whirring with activity and clamoring chatter. How was she supposed to find the right "someone" who'd been ordered to meet her? That is, if someone *was* meeting her, and this job offer wasn't a mean-spirited hoax.

She found a place to pause beside a pillar where she'd be safely out of the way of frenzied travelers and beeping conveyance vehicles. Anxiety roiled in her belly as she scanned the ordered chaos, wondering how her escort would find her? Had he—or she—been shown the picture she'd sent to Mr. Varos before the wedding was arranged? Would he—or she—even show? The thought of coming all this way just to be left standing at the airport like a potted palm made her shudder.

"How did I get here—and why am I here, at all?" she muttered. Slipping the strap of her carry-on bag off her shoulder, she lay the case on the tile. For the thousandth time she went over the whole bizarre situation in her mind. First she'd rejected Mr. Varos. Then he'd called and offered her the opportunity to refurbish the mansion. When he'd hung up, she still hadn't actually said she'd come. She remained torn most of the week, first thinking she couldn't possibly agree, then deciding she couldn't possibly refuse.

She'd even looked up old photographs of the Varos mansion, when it had been The Gladingstone House in its turn-of-the-century heyday. The estate had been gorgeous. She knew standing before the real thing would take her breath away. *If* she decided to return to San Francisco.

If? Getting this chance was like getting tapped for the Olympics. Not an offer easily rejected—since such an opportunity was the absolute epitome of everything she'd ever hoped to do in her life.

Aside from that, she *owed* Mr. Varos. She knew she could do a good job. *She could do an excellent job.* And she would, because of all she had at stake. She had a huge broken promise to make up for. And that was above and beyond everything this job would do for her career.

She experienced another surge of nervous anticipation and smoothed her navy linen jacket. Her high heels pinched a little, but that was a small price to pay. She'd dressed for success, wanting to make a top-notch impression. Though she wouldn't see Mr. Varos, himself, he would hear about the project. She didn't want a single, solitary negative word getting back to him, about her work or herself. She would be a professional from the tip of her head to the ends of her aching toes. No mealymouthed behavior this time. Nothing would go wrong. She would prove to Mr. Varos that his faith in her was not misplaced.

She shifted her weight in her all-business shoes, trying to make the ache in her toes go away. Eagerly she scanned everyone who passed by, her smile hopeful and expectant. Almost pleading, *"Please be from Mr. Varos's staff!"*

After forty-five gut-wrenching minutes, her feet were killing her and her face muscles hurt from all the futile smiling. She was near the extreme end of the terminal wing. Everyone had left the area who'd been on her flight. Even stragglers whose loved ones arrived late were gone.

A smattering of strangers ambled by on their way to the final couple of gates, and a handful of early arrivals for the next flight out of Kalli's gate drifted up and milled around, waiting for a departure still an hour and a half away. Even so, in view of Kalli's state of mind, she felt very *alone* as she loitered by a pillar she was beginning to hate. She wished she'd opted to vegetate sitting down. It would have been just as easy to be ignored and forgotten in a seated position as it had been standing around in those cruel new shoes.

She didn't want to believe the offer was a joke, that Mr. Varos had never intended to give her the assignment. She wanted to believe there was a good explanation, and if she was patient someone would arrive. Possibly the traffic was bad.

She could always call his office. She had the number. The only question was, how long did she wait before she sought out a telephone? Why hadn't she bought a cellular? Everybody else in the universe had one. That was the very next thing she promised herself she'd do. After this job—or this—prank.

She sighed, worried and tired. What if somebody had been there but didn't recognize her from the picture. Her hair had been shorter then. At a loss, she mumbled, ''Maybe I should have made a big sign that said I'm Kalli Angelis.''

''That's not necessary,'' came a masculine voice from so nearby she jumped and clasped a hand over her heart. Spinning she saw him. Tall, straight and powerfully built. A shaft of sunlight gave a luminous radiance to earth-colored hair, and it gleamed like a dark halo. She stared wordlessly.

His face was angular, his features pleasantly strong. Sunglasses veiled his eyes, which was too bad, since a shadowy half smile rode a surprisingly sensuous mouth. She wished she could know what his eyes said, since his lips seemed to find her vaguely amusing—in an annoying way. Maybe having to pick her up had unhinged his schedule. ''Miss Angelis, I'm your ride,'' he said, in that same, low drawl. A rough-sexy edge to his voice made his innocent statement sound downright naughty, but she sensed the erotic delivery was completely uncontrived.

Dressed as he was, in jeans, rust colored Henley shirt and work boots, he didn't look like a man who contrived anything. His attitude and attire fairly shouted, ''I am what I am, so deal with it!'' She experienced an appreciative shiver along her spine. She didn't know what she'd expected, but it certainly hadn't been anything like this hunk.

He cleared his throat. Though she couldn't see his eyes, she could see his lips, which indicated the irritation was winning out over amusement. His rankled perusal, even masked by dark glasses, made it clear he expected some kind of response. Preferably this year.

Belatedly she nodded. ''Oh—my ride? Great. Thanks.''

''My pleasure.'' As he scooped up her carry-on bag, his lips kicked downward at the corners divulging the unvarnished truth. *It was really no pleasure at all.*

She experienced a twinge. ''I—I thought I'd been abandoned—you're so late.''

''Am I?'' He pursed his lips. ''Perhaps I got the arrival time wrong.'' He indicated the direction and began to walk off with her bag. ''This way.''

After an instant's surprised hesitation by his abrupt departure, she scurried up beside him. "Uh—well, at least you're here, now. That's what counts. I gather you're giving me a ride to Mr. Varos's estate?"

He canted his head in her direction. "Good guess."

She made a disgruntled face at his surly attitude, but he didn't see it, since he'd turned away. His strides were long and she had to run to keep up, which was torture on her pinched feet. "Is there some kind of huge hurry?"

"Not huge."

He didn't look at her or slow his pace. She eyed his hawkish profile with growing aggravation. "Really?" she shot back. He wasn't the only one who knew how to be surly. "Then how fast would we be running if it *was* huge?"

This time when he glanced her way, he slowed. "Am I walking too fast?"

"Not if we're entered in a marathon. But if you don't want to lose me in the airport, you *might* be. These are not exactly jogging shoes." She indicated her high heels, her expression admonishing.

She couldn't tell if he even bothered to glance at her feet, but she could detect bunching in his jaw muscles. "Sorry." He resumed his trek, only infinitesimally slower than before. A telling indication of how little he cared about her feelings.

"Gee whiz." She sprinted along beside him. "This is so much better. Thanks."

"My pleasure."

She scowled. He had a way of saying "My pleasure" that sounded suspiciously like "Go to hell."

"We'll need to—go to baggage claim," she said, sorry to hear herself panting like a thirsty basset hound. "Do you know—the way to baggage claim?"

He flicked a harsh look her way. At least she thought he did, but he didn't say anything. When he turned a corner, she skidded around it, too.

"So—what do you do when you're not fetching people at airports?" she asked, trying to make conversation.

"I mind my own business."

She stumbled, but regained her balance in time to keep from falling on her backside.

Breaking into a sprint, she caught up with him. "Well, that—that was *rude!*" She grabbed his wrist, sturdy and warm and masculine. She didn't know what she expected, but touching his flesh had a startling effect on her.

She swallowed. "I presume you work for Mr. Varos?" She said it in a tone meant to threaten that she would tattle about his boorishness, and quite possibly get him fired. She would never actually do such a thing, but this bad-mannered lout didn't need to know. "Because, he should be informed about how you treat people!"

Her escort came to a stop so abruptly she was a step beyond him before she realized it. She whirled back as his head tilted down, making it plain he was focusing on her hand clutching his arm. With a slight twist of his wrist, he separated them. Sweeping the recently freed appendage outward, he indicated the nearest baggage carousel. "Pick a bag, Miss Angelis."

"That won't be hard," she said, sweeping her own arm out. "There's just the *one* left!"

"Why don't I get that for you, ma'am." He gave a slight, mocking salute and turned away.

She crossed her arms and scowled at the back of his head, deciding she could be as closemouthed as he. A few minutes later she was strapped into a sleek, two-seater sports car. Her belongings had barely fit into the trunk. Another indication that he hadn't put a great deal of thought or care into this assignment.

As they sped northward, she found herself wondering about this delivery guy who'd been delegated to drive her to the remote Varos estate. She hoped it wasn't too remote, since sitting beside a glowering grouch was not the most fun she'd ever had.

There were positives about the ride, though. The sun felt good on her face, mild and friendly—not a thing like the short-tempered sphinx at the wheel. She lay her head back to enjoy the cool breeze and the benevolent sunshine. After a time, she realized they were crossing the Golden Gate Bridge, a symphony in steel, recognizable around the world. She sat up to take in the spectacular view of ocean and the cliffs off to the west. On the eastern side, green hills spread out all around. Far below, lay San Francisco Bay, with its teeming marinas. Sailboats glided among verdant islands that dotted blue water. The tangy scent of the sea rose up to greet her and she inhaled, enjoying the extraordinary experience.

She looked at her unfriendly companion and her smile evaporated. His neatly trimmed hair ruffled in the breeze. Glossy brown tendrils skidded and cavorted across his forehead. Bathed in early-afternoon sunlight the way he was, Kalli had to admit he was deliciously handsome—except for the cantankerous set of his jaw. There was a coiled strength about him, a rugged vitality, that both attracted and troubled her. Clearly this was a man who didn't give a tinker's damn about what she or anyone else thought about him.

Unfortunately, even as moody and grouchy as he was, there was something in him that sent tremors of feminine attraction zinging through her veins. She hated conceding such a thing even for one fleeting instant. Why did she have to find him tempting? He was a rude, tight-lipped jerk. The sooner he dropped her off and drove out of her life, the better she'd like it.

Sitting more erect, she decided she might as well attempt conversation one more time. It was better than admiring the gleam of his hair or the appealing ridge of his cheekbones.

"Nice convertible," she said. "Is it yours?"

"It's one of the Varos cars."

She nodded. That made sense. Not many people would be able to afford a snazzy vehicle like this. "So you're the chauffeur?"

"Sometimes."

"When you're not teaching the sensitivity training seminars?" she asked, trying to get a rise out of him. She wasn't sure why. Maybe it was because he could so easily get one out of her.

She didn't succeed. He merely stared at the highway. No, that wasn't totally accurate. He flexed one hand. She wondered if that meant he was clutching the steering wheel so tightly his hands were cramping. Ha! Good! If he had to exasperate her then she might as well return the favor.

"Do you have a name?" she asked, "Or are you an android with a glitch in your disposition software?"

His square jaw tensed, and she canted her head in his direction, fascinated by the play of light and shadow on his sharply defined features. As soon as she realized she was admiring him, she shifted to glare at the highway. When he didn't respond, she had no choice but to reroute her glare in his direction. Cupping her hands around her mouth, she shouted, "I said, do you have a name, or—"

"I heard you, Miss Angelis."

She continued to glower at him, but refused to say another word. If he chose to be a boor, it was his business. She didn't care if he had a name or not.

After another ponderous accumulation of minutes, he startled her with, "Some people call me Pal."

When she stopped reeling from shock that he'd actually spoken to her, she stared at him. "No kidding?" She made a disbelieving face. "No doubt due to your laugh-a-minute personality?"

He said nothing more, just drove.

Pal? It didn't fit with the obnoxious image she had of the man. She decided to delve into the possible spin-offs of Pal. Out loud. If nothing else, her droning on might annoy him, and that was dandy with her. "One thing we can cross off the list is 'Pal' as in buddy or friend.

The reasons for ruling them out are so laughably obvious I won't even go there."

She wanted to peek at him to see if his jaw muscles reacted to that dig, but she resisted. "Let's see. Pal..." She scrunched up her forehead. "This is a hard one." She peered at him. "Care to give me a hint?"

His only reaction was to check the rearview mirror and slide into the passing lane. What was this? Speeding up in order to get rid of her that much quicker? Her antagonism kicked into high gear along with the sports car. "I've got it!" She snapped her fingers and beamed at his profile. "You're nicknamed after the palm crab! The reasons for that would be self-explanatory. And—no, wait, *Paltry!* That's it!" She clapped her hands together with glee. "Paltry—meaning wretched, pettifogging and *contemptible!*"

She presented him with a victorious grin. Proud of herself and her wit, she was positive she'd showed ol' "Pal" here, a thing or two about exactly who he was dealing with. "Am I right, or am I right?" she asked, a jubilant lilt in her tone.

"Pettifogging?" He stared at her for an instant as he downshifted at an exit.

"It's a *word,*" she shot back, her triumphant smile intact. "It means trashy, shoddy—"

"Pal is short for Palikaraki. A nickname from my grandfather. "

"Palikaraki?" Kalli's smile mutated into a confused frown. "But—but that's Greek for 'little hero.'"

The sports car sped along a hilly country road winding through a forest of pines and California live oak. As her companion drove, he slowly and deliberately lowered his head, then raised it. Kalli had to assume the move was a nod.

"Little hero?" She gave him another once-over. "Well, without getting into the delusions of your grandfather—does that mean you're, by some freaky chance—Greek?"

Again he did that slow up and down thing with his head, another positive, if mute, response.

"I'm Greek, too." She eyed him with curiosity, concluding it wouldn't be strange for Mr. Varos to have other Greeks in his employ. There were probably lots of Greeks in

California. As a matter of fact, it would make perfect sense. On two levels.

If Mr. Varos would go to the extreme of marrying a woman he didn't know just because she was Greek, he would surely hire Greeks. And that solved the other burning question. How anybody as bad-tempered as Pal, here, could even *get* a job—certainly only by playing the Greek card.

"And I thought 'little hero' was just a good guess." He glanced her way. "I'm disappointed."

Her annoyance flared at his taunt. "You're disappointed?" she said. "*You're* disappointed! Well, Pal, let me tell you about disappointment!"

They came to a stop before a towering wrought-iron gate. Beautiful and ornate, it depicted scrolls, gilded flowers and acanthus leaves. The iron barrier was set in massive stone posts, topped with elaborate wrought-iron lanterns.

Kalli noticed Pal turn and glance up to his left. She followed his gaze, but didn't see anything at first. After a minute of puzzled scrutinizing, she spotted a small camera mounted unobtrusively in a niche on the pillar, nearly hidden by branches of a towering cedar.

After a short pause, the gate began to open to the accompaniment of a low mechanical hum.

Kalli was surprised Pal didn't have to say anything. "Do they have eyeball prints of every employee, or something?"

He drove through the open gate without responding to her wisecrack.

She shifted to look back, and watched as the magnificent iron blockade made its ponderous return trek to block access to the Varos property.

"You were telling me something about disappointment, Miss Angelis?"

"*Oh!*" She jumped in surprise, something Pal seemed everlastingly good at making her do. She couldn't recall reacting so powerful to any other man who merely initiated a conversation. What was it about Pal that could coax her to the brink of a conniption fit.

"Disappointment?" She shook her head, trying to refocus. The sight of the majestic gate had reminded her why she was here, and she experienced a surge of excitement about the project for the first time since—well, since the proposition of refurbishing the property had been made via Mr. Varos's lawyers, when the marriage deal was being hammered out.

She swallowed, her throat dry. It was hard to believe she'd even considered such a daft idea as an arranged marriage. ''Oh—right. Disappointment.''

She strained to see over the treetops, and thought she spied a spire here and a chimney there. She would see the house very soon. Her heartbeat sped up and she gave Pal a disgruntled peek. She would be rid of her disagreeable escort, too.

That knowledge made her bold.

''I'll tell you about disappointment!'' she said, allowing her resentment free access to her mouth. ''Disappointment is being picked up at the airport by a big, grouchy bear. Disappointment is having to spend these past two, unending hours with a snarling sorehead. And *real* disappointment is discovering that same big, grouchy bear of a sorehead is *Greek,* a cruel, ugly blot on an otherwise *wonderful* people!''

Belligerent and full of vinegar, she leaned toward him, hopeful her aggressive slant would rattle him just a little. ''That's *real* disappointment, buster!'' She flicked him hard on the arm. ''That's *bottom-line* disappointment—Pal!''

They headed around a bend and up an incline. Out of the corner of her eye, Kalli saw a flash of color that wasn't part of the verdant landscape. She turned instinctively as the Varos mansion rose before her amid a paradise of blooming shrubs, flowers and the heavy perfume of wisteria.

She sucked in a breath, experiencing a warm, rosy feeling she could only describe as love-at-first-sight. The Victorian residence had a fairy-tale quality—a delicate castle, created from a romantic marriage of brick, stone and wood.

It was a three-storied cornucopia of Victorian elements, cleverly mingled from its gables, dormers and Palladian windows to the wraparound graystone veranda and lofty tower. The dwelling was unique and whimsical—a charming reflection of childhood fantasies and make-believe.

"Oh," she cried, her passion for her work cresting and overflowing. "There's so much—so much—" Her voice broke, so she waved a broad arch in the air, indicating its potential. The home was not merely plaster, board and stone to Kalli. It was a living, breathing entity—a being with a soul and character, who, over the years, had been wronged and degraded with regrettable paint choices and injurious additions.

To be given the chance to save such a treasure, to restore it to its original glory, would be a dream-come-true to anyone in her profession. Kalli gawked, overwhelmed that Mr. Varos would entrust such an undertaking into her care.

The mansion began to quiver before her eyes, then blurred. As the sports car pulled to a stop, she blinked, dislodging tears of gratitude.

"I gather the house is a real, bottom-line disappointment?"

Pal's cynical remark coming so near her ear made her cry out. She jerked to glare at him. "You scared me!" She swiped at the tears with the back of her hand, not even slightly embarrassed that he'd seen her cry. Some things were simply worth crying over, and this superb mansion was one of them.

He shifted to lounge against the leather and draped an arm across the back of her seat. "I thought you knew I was here," he said, his tone dripping with mockery. "I'm sorry."

If she'd ever heard a you're-a-pain-in-the-neck antiapology, that was it. She bounced around, presenting her back to him and focusing on the house. Her hands trembling with anger, she busily straightened her suit jacket and finger-combed her hair.

"You really should be sorry, you know!" She spun back to glower at him. "And to answer your question, no. The house is not a disappointment. It's wonderful. I'm deeply moved that Mr. Varos wants me to refurbish it. There's such innate beauty, such graceful transcendency. With the right creative hand, the right artistic eye, Mr. Varos's home could become a work of art."

He lifted his chin, a clear indication his attention had moved in the direction of the house, somewhere behind and above her. She gave him a hard, offended look. Why was she bothering to explain? He wasn't listening. Besides, this insensitive part-time-chauffeur-handyman-all-round-disagreeable-underling couldn't possibly understand how aesthetics could stir the receptive spirit.

"Oh—never mind." Shaking her head, she indicated the rear of the car. "If you'll pop the trunk, I'll get my bags. I wouldn't want to keep you."

"I'll get your bags, miss."

This new male voice came from behind and slightly above her. She jerked around. A trim, white-haired man in black stood midway down the brick staircase that led to the arched entry. The servant wore white gloves and a reserved, yet welcoming, smile. Kalli heard a click as the car trunk popped open.

Without waiting for further evidence of permission to retrieve her bags, the man descended the steps and headed to the rear of the car. Kalli pushed open her door and got out, only partly in a desire to help with her bags. One unruly portion of her brain had an urge to turn and gaze just once more at—well, it was a stupid urge, and she fought it by leaping from the convertible.

As she shut the car door, another man emerged from the shadows of the wide, covered porch. This new arrival was tall and thin, wore a dark suit, green-and-navy striped tie, and carried a black leather briefcase. His long, pale face and receding hairline seemed familiar. Kalli paused to scrutinize him, digging into her memory. When his glance shifted to meet hers, he came to a dead stop, his eyes going wide. *That was it!* That startled doe look told her exactly were she'd seen him before. She gasped, wagging an accusing finger at him. ''But you said you wouldn't be here!''

She didn't like the panic in her voice. She'd meant to sound stern, all business. She noticed her finger, still wagging in his direction. It looked so moronic, she dropped her hand to her side, struggling to keep her lower lip from trembling. She felt rotten about what she'd done to Mr. Varos, and she was still acting badly. Working to regain her poise, she made herself breathe evenly.

''I—I'm just leaving.'' The man she'd jilted walked down the remainder of the steps to the brick driveway.

Kalli felt wretched. How could she have shouted, especially considering he'd offered her this wonderful job? She hurried over to him and took his free hand in both of hers. "Oh, Mr. Varos, you must think I'm an ungrateful shrew." She pumped his cool, limp fingers. "Thank you so much for this chance. I'll do my very, very utmost to make your home the showpiece it deserves to be. I'm thrilled to be here. You're too kind, and I'll never, ever forget—"

"Miss Angelis," Pal cut in. "If you'll kindly release my assistant, he's on a tight schedule."

Kalli stopped pumping and opened her mouth to ask Pal what he was babbling about, but he'd turned to the pale man whose hand she clutched. "Charles, I left the Magnason contracts on my desk. Express mail them this afternoon. Then drive the Boxster to the garage. It needs to be detailed."

"Yes, sir." The pale man's gaze darted from Kalli to Pal and back to Kalli.

Pal held out the car keys but when they weren't immediately retrieved, he frowned, pointedly staring down at the pallid hand Kalli gripped with all her strength. "Don't cut off his circulation, Miss Angelis. Charles needs those fingers. He types one hundred words a minute."

Pal lifted away his sunglasses to reveal darkly fringed eyes the color of smoke. Those eyes captured her gaze and her breath. Without looking away, he signaled the butler. "Take Miss Angelis' bags inside, Belkin. She's thrilled to be here."

Those lips Kalli had found disturbingly sensuous curled in a wicked grin and he winked, the most brazen, most calculated act she'd ever seen. Her reaction was just short of apoplexy.

"What—what's going on here?" she asked in a fragile whisper. "Isn't this…" She jerked to stare accusingly at the pale man whose hand she held. "But—aren't you…?"

"No, ma'am. I'm Charles Early." He made a sickly effort to smile. "I'm pleased to meet you."

"But—but…" Horrified, she gaped at Pal. The truth trying to seep into her brain was too terrible to contemplate. "But you can't be…"

He bowed his head slightly, as though being introduced at a formal gathering. "Nikolos

Varos, at your service.'' Slipping the convertible's keys into Charles's coat pocket, Niko kept her gaze locked with his, his grin crooked. ''It's my pleasure to meet you—at last.''

Even in her dazed stupor, Kalli was hit between the eyes with his brazen insolence. He'd made a fool of her and he loved it. As far as Nikolos Varos was concerned, their alliance was so completely opposite from a pleasure, she could feel the antagonism pulsating through her as surely and painfully as if she were standing on a downed electric cable. He didn't like her, didn't want to be in the same state with her. So why...

He took her arm, short-circuiting her thought processes. ''Allow me to show you to your room.''

Groping around in her brain for balance and sanity, she belatedly managed to yank from his hold. ''You promised you wouldn't be here!''

Niko stood a step below her, but she still had to look up to scan his expression. ''Actually,'' he corrected, ''Charles said he wouldn't be here.'' One dark brow rose as he observed her, his smile gone. ''More to the point, you promised to marry me. Why are you still Miss Angelis?''

The blunt rebuke broadsided Kalli. She felt dizzy and she couldn't catch her breath. *This wouldn't work.* She couldn't be here, couldn't stay. Suddenly ice-cold, she hugged herself. ''This is impossible, Mr. Varos,'' she whispered. Her ex-fiancé might not have a broken heart because of her rejection, but his blood-thirsty streak was all too real. ''Under the circumstances, I—I can't stay.''

Niko's brow furrowed for an instant, then his features became unreadable. ''It's your decision, of course,'' he said in that rough-sexy drawl. ''Most people in your profession would endure hell on earth to get a prestigious opportunity like this.'' He indicated the house. ''Look at it again, Miss Angelis. Tell me I'm wrong.''

She didn't have to look. She knew he was right. In all her experience she'd never seen a more spectacular example of the American Victorian style. With proper refurbishing, the grand edifice could be a masterpiece of the period. How many people got the chance to help create a masterpiece?

Her sense of loss was like a molten steel weight in her belly and she had to fight to keep from bursting into tears. She shook her head, befuddled and stupid. She wished she could be anywhere else, but she knew her cowardly behavior toward Mr. Varos had to end. Choking back a sob, she resolutely met his gaze. "Since you obviously detest me, why would you offer such a five-star job—*to me?* It doesn't make sense."

"It's very simple, Miss Angelis." A knife-edged chill clung to his words. "Because I keep my promises."

CHAPTER THREE

THAT stinging insult hadn't been Niko's most shining hour. He watched his ex-fiancée wince. Odd, he didn't feel quite the surge of satisfaction he'd thought he would.

She opened her mouth, but before she could respond, he grasped her elbow and steered her up the steps into the mansion's foyer.

"But, Mr. Var—"

"By the way," he cut in, uncompromising in his plan to teach his fickle ex-fiancée a lesson about breaking pledges. "Regarding your gushing thanks earlier—you're quite welcome. It's my pleasure." He knew his forbidding expression would underscore the lie.

She startled him when she yanked from his hold and spun to confront him. "Will *you* be here the whole time?" Her eyes, a captivating lavender-gray, sparked with animosity and distress. Though her face was the perfect oval he'd admired in her picture, he was becoming acquainted with her chin of iron determination.

At the moment, it jutted accusingly. Her jet-black hair flowed out in soft waves from a center part. Disheveled from the convertible ride, the thick mane gleamed, a dusky aura around her flushed face.

She looked a little crazed, in an engaging way. His heated reaction to a mass of glossy hair and a blush made him furious with himself. He didn't like this woman. She might be attractive but she was flighty and couldn't be trusted to keep important promises. This flaw in her character had caused him no end of embarrassment. He hadn't been able to go anywhere in the city without being ribbed that he'd been ''left at the altar,'' not to mention all the pointing and staring from strangers.

''Well,'' she demanded, aiming that lethal little chin at his heart. ''Are you planning to be here?''

With a studied nonchalance he didn't feel, Niko shrugged his hands into his jeans pockets. ''If you'll recall, I'm on vacation.''

''Don't you have a place in town?'' Her voice had gone high-pitched and shrill. She was truly alarmed about this turn of events. That knowledge sent a rush of malevolent pleasure through him. "My place in town needs repair work," he said. "I'll be staying here for the duration."

"Duration?" she squeaked.

"Three weeks."

Her horrified expression almost made him smile.

"But—but that's how long..." Her voice broke and she didn't finish. They both knew she needed to be there that long. He watched her swallow several times, obviously trying to get her voice under control. "You lied to me," she whispered at last.

"Did I?" He challenged her with his most innocent expression.

"Yes!" She glared, clearly attempting to kill him with that look. "When you said you wouldn't be here. You lied!"

"Charles told you *he* wouldn't be here."

"But he—*you*—allowed me to assume—"

"What you assume, Miss Angelis, is hardly my fault."

She blinked, then her stare grew wider, as though she'd had a distasteful thought. "Do you think you need to keep an eye on me? Is that why you're staying? You don't trust me to get the job done?''

That wasn't the reason, but the idea had merit. ''Why would I need to do that?'' he asked. ''When have I ever known you to break your word?''

She opened her lips, but plainly shaken by his direct shot, couldn't seem to form words. Niko gave her no time to recoup and dropped a bomb. ''The fact is, this is a beautiful piece of property. I own it, so why shouldn't I stay? After all, this was supposed to be my honeymoon.''

He heard her guttural moan and knew he'd drawn blood. ''This is—this is bad!'' She rubbed her temples as though trying to ward off a headache. ''I can't take your insults for three weeks. I can't even take them for three minutes.'' The butler came down the steps. At the sound of his approach, she whirled. ''Excuse me, sir.'' She waved frantically. ''Please, get my bags. I'm leaving.''

''I thought you'd bail out, again,'' Niko said, baiting her.

''Bail out?'' She whirled, giving him another direct shot with that lethal chin. ''How dare you say I'm bailing out! It's nothing of the sort! I simply won't subject myself to your mocking and insulting, and if you even thought I might, you're—you're demented!''

''I never thought you would,'' he lied. He knew damn well what she would do, and stared her down as she blustered and stammered, trying to convince herself she wasn't a quitter. She might have been able to bail out on him and their marriage, but she had never met him. Her job was another thing entirely. She knew her job, and was passionate about her work. He'd done enough research on her to be sure of that. She would stay, or Niko Varos wasn't the hotshot international financial consultant people thought he was.

''N-nothing—'' she stammered, ''not this house, not *any* house—is worth—'' she indicated the faded grandeur of an entry hall, decorated in retro-fifties camp ''—worth putting up with your—with your...''

Her glance trailed her broad gesture. Before she completed her sweep, she stilled. Her lips sagged and her distressed expression changed into one of abject horror, as though she only now absorbed the scandalous violation done to this mansion and its proud Victorian roots.

The fine old wood floor had been painted in a green-and-yellow checkerboard pattern. The wallpaper bore a splashy, modern art look Niko assumed were supposed to be untidy piles of pipe. The dangling light fixture consisted of three beach-ball-size yellow, plastic orbs. Beneath them sat a sprawling amoeba-shaped table with a marbled mirror top, supported by spindly metal legs.

She covered her mouth with both hands and strangled a gasp as she staggered around in a circle. Niko watched as her glance fell to a side wall. A round, molded plywood table stood between two doors. Atop its indented surface squatted a funky lamp made to resemble a big lightbulb. Kalli bit her lip, her glance skidding to another wall where a yellow, rectangular clock, the size of a breakfast tray dominated.

The clock's hands were disconcertingly off-center. An oversize, red secondhand *tick-tick-ticked* as she stared, wide-eyed. Niko had the sense each jerk of that red, mechanical arm boomed in her head as she suffered, second by painful second. He had to fight a knowing grin as he observed her sluggish, stumbling body language. Only seeing her scream and collapse in a traumatized heap would have made it more obvious she was experiencing a gut-wrenching ache to rescue the place from its gross defilement.

"Cute, isn't it?" he taunted, well aware he was being cruel. "I especially like the lead-pipe motif in the wallpaper."

"Oh—dear heaven..." she whimpered, shaking her head. "It's so—so wrong. It's dreadful."

"But is it dreadful enough to endure a brief captivity in a hell-on-earth?"

She stood with her back to him, her shoulders slightly drooped. He sensed her turmoil and gave her a moment to agonize over the knowledge that beneath layers of wrong-headed embellishments a masterpiece cried out to be liberated. He could almost hear her thinking, *I could save this house. I must save it!* He pursed his lips to suppress a shrewd grin.

The thud of his butler's footsteps drew his gaze once again to the central staircase. The liveried man descended, carrying a suitcase and shoulder tote.

Niko's attention slid to his angsting ex. She, too, had heard the butler and looked up. Niko waited, silent. At the moment, it would be unwise to remind her of his unwelcome presence. In order for her to make the decision that fit with his ploy, she needed to think of the house and only the house.

"I—uh..."

Niko watched her straighten her shoulders. "I'm sorry." She moved toward the stairs, addressing the butler. "I'm staying, after all." She rushed up the steps and took the bags. "Please show me to my room."

Belkin glanced at his employer, his expression pinched with confusion.

Niko nodded, experiencing a rush of satisfaction. He allowed himself a crafty grin as he watched her trudge, stiff-backed and squeamish, into the lion's den.

Kalli unpacked her bag in a bizarre trancelike state. She walked back and forth from her suitcase to the chartreuse dresser with its aluminum top and side trim and cane inset drawers.

As she put her belongings away her brain screamed, *Three weeks? You've agreed to stay under the same roof with a man who obviously hates you for three whole weeks? What are you using your brain for, Kalli? To keep your skull from imploding?*

After a sound tongue-lashing from the logical section of her cranium, the artistic quarter leaped into the fray and lashed back. *But he was right when he said three weeks in a hell-on-earth would be worth the opportunity to transform this abused Victorian treasure into the monument to American history it should be.*

Reality check, Kalli! The man hates you, and intends to make your life miserable. Are you ready for that?

I don't know! I don't know! Leave me alone! She plunked down on the bed and grabbed handfuls of hair. Closing her fingers into fists, she muttered, ''I know he hates me and wants me to suffer for running out on the wedding. But...''

She scanned the bedroom with its sublime fourteen-foot ceiling. Once, long ago it had been lovely. The original casement windows still held their quaint bull's-eye panes. And she'd seen a glimpse of the original parquet planking, visible in the closet. Green and burnt-umber carpeting, sporting a haphazard hoop-and-cube design, hid the wonderful old floor from view. The room's deep, simply molded baseboards were classically Victorian. The ornate cornices were exemplary, too; but painted the same gray-green as the walls, their splendor was so camouflaged it was all but lost.

Kalli knew the fifties had been a decade of budding space exploration. America's love affair with aeronautical technology brought with it decorating schemes of unornamental flatness, geometric forms and daring color combinations. Kalli had always considered the look airy, sleek, clean and bright. Unfortunately, in the case of this home, someone had heavy-handedly inflicted the retro-fifties veneer on beautiful old Victorian architecture. Rather than sleek and pleasing, the effect was not only criminally inappropriate but erratic and unnerving.

Could restoring this sleeping goddess to her virginal glory be worth three weeks of guaranteed hell, tormented and badgered by a vindictive male? She inhaled, her gaze roving over the bedchamber. Her heart swelled as she envisioned all it could be. It would be a sin to run away. The house needed her. On both an emotional level and a professional level, she would regret leaving for the rest of her life. ''Yes,'' she breathed, experiencing a renewed flow of courage. ''Yes! It's worth anything Mr. Varos might choose to put me through.''

She shoved off the bed, glaring toward the room's chartreuse door. ''If insulting me and making me squirm is your idea of a vacation, Mr. Varos, then do your worst. Go ahead and watch me like a hawk, but you won't find my work wanting. And I won't run away!'' She threw back her head and placed her hands on her hips. ''Because Kalli Angelis is made of sterner stuff than you know. I'll turn this Bitterweed into an American Beauty Rose, no matter how much grief you pile on my head. And you can take *that* to your precious bank!''

Kalli didn't want to waste a minute under Nikolos Varos's roof, so that afternoon she got started, trekking from magnificent room to magnificent room snapping photographs and scribbling copious notes. With each new encounter, she was simultaneously awed and appalled. Obviously Mr. Varos had purchased the place with the furniture included. She couldn't believe he would have recently acquired it, furnished it to match the misguided decor, only to immediately commission someone to have it completely redone. Not unless he had more money than sense. Which was a possibility, she supposed. *Somebody* had inflicted this travesty on the lovely old home.

Though she worked with dogged single-mindedness, she could always tell when Niko was near. So much for her reputed single-mindedness. Even his momentary loitering in a neighboring hallway short-circuited her ability to think, let alone be creative.

Every time she heard the distinctive rap of his step or sniffed his woodsy aftershave, her focus grew hazy. Architectural details became nondescript and peculiarly irrelevant. What was her problem? Why couldn't she concentrate when he happened by? Was it anxiety? Was she waiting for the other shoe to drop and wondering exactly how deafening the explosion would be? Did she expect him to leap out at her and shout *"boo"*? Or douse her with a water hose?

Working to shut her mind to everything but her note-taking, she peeled away a corner of silvered wallpaper to discover the faded remnants of a stunning handmade woodblock design. Even as agitated as she was, Kalli managed an appreciative smile and jotted the information in her workbook. Once again the wondrous reality of her good luck gave her a fleeting reprieve from thoughts of Nikolos Varos and his lurking glower.

The afternoon passed without any shoes dropping or massive explosions. As a matter of fact, he'd said nothing at all to her. He didn't even join her at dinner, so she ate alone in a room that could have housed a double-decker bus. In the overpowering silence she picked at something tasty, exotic and crab-meaty, but she hardly noticed it.

Her interest lay in scanning the dining room. Walls, paneled up to the dado rail, had once been stained a rich walnut, but were now painted a nasty orange. Coordinating wallpaper depicted a psychedelic skirmish of color and design that would have sent Kalli scurrying under the table if the structure hadn't been such a scary, stainless-steel monstrosity. Its brushed serpentine surface was so cold to the touch, Kalli found herself holding her utensils by their extreme ends to keep from making contact.

Twenty molded fiberglass chairs, thinly upholstered in lemon vinyl with skinny metal legs, surrounded the table like half-starved munchkins attempting to hold the slithering beast at bay. She experienced an ironic giggle and mumbled, ''Kalli, you're not in Kansas anymore. You're definitely in Oz.''

She glanced up. Where crystal chandeliers once sparkled in the lofty space between the paneled ceiling and table, tract lighting now dominated. Fuzzy fiberglass cones angled hither and yon, illuminated random snippets of space. Kalli shivered at the chilly severity the room generated. ''If you want my opinion, Mr. Varos,'' she muttered, ''the decor suits you perfectly.''

''Thank you.''

She squealed and jerked. When she turned toward the deep voice, she pressed her hands to her chest. "What are you trying to do, give me a heart attack?"

He ambled through the arched entry, still clad in his jeans, looking more like a hunky handyman who'd arrived to do a repair weld on the table than to play host. "Enjoying the Crab Chantilly?"

She eyed him critically. "Why? Is it poisoned?"

He grinned and took a seat opposite her. "How did we get off to such a poor start, Miss Angelis?"

She lay her forearms on the table and leaned in his direction. "Maybe, because you hate me, and you're having trouble hiding it?"

He sat forward, mimicking her belligerent pose, though his lips remained curved in a grin. "I'm not trying to hide it, Miss Angelis."

She sat back, giving up her attempt at intimidation. No matter how she might try, she knew she couldn't outbelligerent Nikolos Varos. Especially when he could do it so masterfully—and still smile. The look in his smoky eyes was cool and treacherous. A tremor raced along her spine as she recalled thinking the room generated a chilly severity.

How naive she'd been only moments ago. The place seemed grandly welcoming, now, compared to the man with the calculating grin, watching her silently from across the table.

"So," he began, after a nerve-shredding pause. "Beside the fact that the decor suits me, what is your initial impression of my home?"

She didn't like the fact that he'd joined her. Didn't like the cynical half smile that screamed his contempt. But she was a professional, and he was—at least on the surface—asking a business question. Shoring up the cracks in her emotions, she opted to rise above sniping level. She cleared her throat and placed her hands in her lap. That way she could squeeze them into fists and he wouldn't know. "Actually," she began, then swallowed to clear the nervous wobble from her tone. "Actually, Mr. Varos, I have no—"

"Niko," he said, lounging back.

She blinked, startled. "What?"

"I said, Niko." He looked away for a moment and motioned someone forward. She followed his gaze. A servant approached holding a plate of steaming food and she experienced a spike of agitation. Was Mr. Varos joining her? Had he planned his arrival to make sure he was insultingly late? Another server followed close behind the first, carrying a tray of miscellany. Her host's gaze returned to snag hers. "Call me Niko, Miss Angelis. I insist."

She felt an uncomfortable certainty that he expected her to extend him the same privilege, but she couldn't bring herself to offer it. The emotional distance of calling him Mr. Varos was more in keeping with how she wanted their relationship to be.

She'd thought of him as Niko when she'd had visions of them—married. Her fantasies had included such phrases as, "I'd like you to meet Niko, my husband," and "Niko, darling, thank you for the roses," or "Niko, dear, please pass me the cream." How ridiculous and adolescent all that seemed now—now that she'd met the man. Not the kind and fun-loving person her grandfather had described, but a vengeful, smirking brute.

Calling him Niko seemed too intimate, considering the way they'd become unengaged, and his offensive attitude toward her. She didn't like to think about it, but the very sound of his given name sent a shaft of renewed guilt charging through her.

Maybe she'd brought out the vengeful brute in him. Maybe he was relatively nice to people who didn't jilt him on his wedding day. She swallowed, trying to dislodge a lump in her throat. But there was nothing to be done about that, now. She'd dumped him flat and she couldn't take it back. She wouldn't want to— except the *way* she'd dumped him. That had been rash and thoughtless, even taking into consideration her grief over Grandpa Chris's death.

She felt uneasy and angry, too—both at herself and at him, for ever considering an arranged marriage. No! She could never call him Niko. Not in a million years. The very idea conjured up too much emotional baggage, too many guilty, uncomfortable memories. It was out of the question.

When his dinner had been set before him along with silverware, cup and saucer and silver coffeepot, he took up his fork and glanced her way. "And what would you like me to call you?"

"Uh—look…" She experienced a stab of panic. "There's nothing wrong with retro-fifties decor." She had no idea how her mind hopped and skidded to that topic. Still, the change of subject was as good a way as any to stall until she had her refusal to call him Niko worked out in businesslike, noninflammatory words.

"I've seen lovely homes done in that style. But mid-twentieth century modernism and Victorian don't mix. At least I don't think they do, but I'm a purist. That's why—" her brain worked a mile a minute, struggling to phrase this properly, at the same time groping for a polite way to reject him…again "—when I said the decor was perfect for you, I didn't necessarily mean—"

"Yes, you did, Miss Angelis," he interrupted, pouring himself a cup of coffee. With a questioning lift of an eyebrow he asked, "Would you care for a refill?"

She shook her head, her cheeks fiery with mortification. He was right, of course. She *had* meant to be insulting. But darn the man, when she'd said it she didn't know he could hear her. Skulking at the door was unfair. Why was it

that the one time she hadn't detected his nearness was the time she had to open her big
mouth?

"Why don't I call you Kalli?" he suggested, his expression inquisitive, in a sly way.
"No need to be formal."

She scooped up a forkful of her food and
took a bite. Another delaying tactic, but not
nearly long enough. What if she set the cur-
tains on fire? That would be a better stall.
Ultimately, the problem of whether he called
her Kalli or Miss Angelis would be solved,
since she would be rotting away in some
prison on an arson conviction, and he would
have no need to call her anything, ever again.

"After all," he went on, seeming not to notice her continued silence, "if we had actually
married, I'd be calling you Kalli."

She felt another swift jab to her solar plexus.
That did it! Flinching, she slammed down her
fork, incensed at his continued harassment.
"Look, Mr. Varos, I know you're mad at me,
and you have every right. I shouldn't have broken my promise the way I did. Feel free to be
as furious as you care to be, for as long as you
like. I apologize! I apologize with ever fiber of

my being. If I could take it back, I would. But we both know I can't."

She leaned forward, the flats of her hands on the cold table. Tears welled and she blinked them back, struggling to keep her voice even. "Mr. Varos, considering your feelings about me—well, to put it bluntly, you and I are *not* friends. We both know you don't like me or trust me. So harass and belittle me to your heart's content if it will salve your wounded pride, but don't expect me to call you Niko."

She shoved up to stand, almost upending her chair in the process. "As for what you may call me, I prefer Miss Angelis." She had a hard time holding eye contact, but she made herself. "If you'll excuse me, I intend to go to my room and get some sleep so I can start bright and early tomorrow. I'm going to get this job done—and done well—as quickly as humanly possible. The sooner I never see you again, Mr. Varos, the happier we'll both be," she sucked in a much-needed breath, then added gravely, "Are we clear?"

He lounged there, watching her for the longest moment of Kalli's life. His expression was contemplative, with only the slightest downturn of his lips. Finally he nodded. ''You've made yourself very clear,'' he said quietly.

She crash-landed off her adrenaline high and felt sick to her stomach and mushy in the knees. What had she just done? Was there one single word in that shrewish outburst that had been businesslike and noninflammatory? She would eat the stainless-steel table if there was. She'd *gladly* eat it. Talk about cutting off your nose to spite your face. And had any apology in the history of apologies been shouted less apologetically? Was that any way to make amends? What was wrong with her? She never shouted at people, especially when she was apologizing. Why did this man drive her to the brink of insanity?

Not only had her apology been unforgivably rude, but what of her work? Refurbishing this mansion was the chance of a lifetime and in a fit of temper she'd thrown it out the window.

Fighting a need to burst into tears over her rashness, she crossed her arms before her, hoping her bravado would hide her misery. ''So— so I'm fired, right?'' *It's better this way,* she told herself. *I might miss out on a career-*

making opportunity, but I won't have to put up with Nikolos Varos's tyranny!

Placing an arm across the back of an adjacent chair, Niko motioned toward the door with the casual wag of his fingers. It was the most trifling dismissal she'd ever witnessed. "Sweet dreams, Miss Angelis."

She hesitated, blinking in bafflement. "So—so, I *am* fired?"

He watched her with a critical squint. "Is that what your employers usually say when they fire you?"

She recoiled at his sarcasm. "I've never been fired in my life!"

He pursed his lips, continuing to hold her prisoner with his narrowed stare. "Well," he said at last, "just so you'll know, sweet dreams is not code for you're fired." His lips quirked suspiciously. "But deep down, you want me to fire you, don't you, Miss Angelis?"

She was so torn she didn't know what she wanted, deep down or otherwise. But she had to admit, her life would be instantly easier if he did. She canted her head this way and that, trying to form an answer that was even vaguely sensible.

After what seemed like an hour in the distressing stillness, he leaned forward and took up his fork. "Go to bed, Miss Angelis." Focusing on his cooling meal, he added, "I don't intend to make it that easy for you." He flicked her a quick, accusing glance. "Remember, you can always quit," he said, thinly. "You're good at that."

CHAPTER FOUR

IF KALLI had any lingering notion of quitting and running home to Kansas, Niko's most recent verbal slap squashed it flat. Drat the man for his everlasting skepticism. She would stay now, even if the house burned down around her. How dare he call her a quitter. *Anybody* would resent being treated the way he treated her, and would have every right to pack up and leave. *Quitter, indeed!*

Her old nemesis, Guilt, tapped her on the shoulder, reminding her that Niko's skepticism, at least where her promises were concerned, was based on experience. She felt a sickening stab in her belly, but made herself go on brushing her hair, preparing for her first, full day working in the mansion.

She made a face at herself in the star-shaped mirror above the aluminum and chartreuse dressing table. "Okay, so he has a right to doubt me." She slammed the brush down on the metal surface. "But he can't expect me to take his vindictiveness like I'm thrilled about it.'' She twisted her hair into an unruly knot, her movements hasty and jerky, then fastened it with a blue clip.

She scanned her attire, surprised to see she'd unconsciously dressed to match her mood. *Blue* jeans, *blue* T-shirt and *blue* sneakers. She was blue, to the max. Blue and regretful and mad, which wasn't a pleasant mix. She needed to scream.

''Enough wallowing,'' she muttered. ''It's time to get to work.'' She pushed up to stand and checked her wristwatch. It was barely six-thirty. She would have sworn it was much later. All her tossing and turning during the night made her feel as if she'd already been there a week.

Since Balderdash, or whatever the butler's name was, had told her breakfast would be served *precisely* at seven o'clock, she decided she had time for a brisk walk around the grounds. She loved summer mornings, with the bright sun heralding a fresh day. When the sun came up it wasn't yet hot, just pleasant warmth against the skin. A brisk, prebreakfast walk would be just the thing to calm her jangled nerves.

Kalli slipped out of her room and headed to the stairs. Bounding down two at a time, she reached the front door and hurried onto the porch. She'd sped down several brick steps before she grasped the fact that she couldn't see the driveway. The whole world seemed to be engulfed in smoke.

For a split second she panicked with visions of the mansion burning to the ground. But almost immediately she realized she couldn't smell smoke. Sniffing the air, she reached out into the damp, chilly haze, hardly able to see beyond her own fingertips. "Fog," she whispered, as the truth hit. "So this is the famous San Francisco fog."

She shivered and hugged herself. The air was not only damp, but cold. Peering over her shoulder she noted even the mansion had grown gray and indistinct. She hunched there in the spooky gloom, freezing, disconcerted and depressed. She couldn't jog in this soup. She didn't know the lay of the land. One false step and she could break her neck.

She rubbed her arms for friction warmth. "S-so much for a booster shot of sunshine." Disappointed and chilled, she trudged inside only to run smack into the man she *least* wanted to run into in the entire world.

"Ouch!" She winced. "My foot!" Stumbling a step back, she dropped unceremoniously to the foyer's painted floor and rubbed her squished toes. She looked up. From her lowly vantage point her ex-fiancé looked twelve feet tall. Not a happy twelve feet tall, either. *He wasn't happy? Was he the one sitting on the floor massaging crushed metatarsal bones?* "What do you have on your feet?" she asked. "Steel boots?"

He looked disturbed, which was normal for him. Yet, she sensed that one-half-of-one percent of his negative attitude was not because he hated the sight of her, but because he'd nearly crippled her. Even that small percentage of regret surprised her. "I'm sorry, Miss Angelis," he said. "I didn't expect anybody to come barreling through the door." He reached out. "Let me help you up."

She eyed the hand with misgivings. After a heartbeat, it came to her that she'd actually been considering his offer. Shoving up to stand, she avoided not only his touch but his eyes. "Don't be ridiculous." She took a look at her watch. Six forty-five. Even if she was a little early, maybe she could get a cup of coffee. If worse came to worst, she could brew it herself. "Will breakfast be served in that big morgue of a dining room?" she asked, keeping her gaze averted.

His lips twitched cynically at her description. "Not in the morgue, in the sunroom, off the kitchen."

She couldn't help seeing irony in his statement. "Sunroom?" she repeated. "So that's where you keep the sun. I wondered, since it's not outside."

She shot him a quick look. He didn't smile. She thought her joke was funny and shrugged off his indifference. What did she care if he found her humor funny or not? "Well, point the way," she said, as coolly as she could. "Or should I just follow the golden glow?"

Still no smile. He indicated the direction with a nod.

She hesitated. "Will you be eating, too?"

This time his lips lifted slightly. Apparently her anxiety over his presence tickled his fancy.

"Would you rather I didn't?" he asked.

She made a face. "You know what *I'd rather*," she said, wishing she could scream, *I'd rather you were in Australia or Afghanistan or, even better, Antarctica!* Instead she repeated, "So, will you be eating?" She was determined to get a straight answer if they had to stand there debating breakfast all day.

"I'm afraid so," he said with that low, sexy drawl. "Over the years eating has become a habit." He indicated the way. "After you, Miss Angelis."

She wanted to insist that if he'd be there she wouldn't eat, but eating had become a habit of hers, too. Last night she'd left the dining room before she'd half finished her meal, and she was hungry. Besides she had a sneaking suspicion Mr. Varos planned to make mealtimes a sizable part of her torture. She might as well get used to it.

She had to learn to deal with the man or starve to death, since she had no intention of whining and begging to be served in her room.

If Mr. Varos thought she would, he'd be supremely disappointed. She didn't plan to behave in any way that would smack of quitting, even when it came to where, and with whom, she ate her meals. Favoring her aching foot, she headed in the direction he indicated.

For all the butler's warnings that breakfast would be served precisely at seven, Kalli was surprised to see the retro Formica and chrome dinette already set for two. Honeydew melon halves brimming with strawberries sat at each place, awaiting their pleasure.

Her troubling companion stunned the life out of her when he walked around behind her to hold her chair. She glared at him as he stood with his hands on the red vinyl back. "What are you doing?" she asked, seeing visions of him ripping the chair out from under her at the last minute.

"Don't you grow gentlemen in Kansas?" he asked, his query accompanied by the quizzical arch of an eyebrow.

"We grow them by the acre. Bushels and bushels of gentlemen." Making sure the chair stayed where it was supposed to, Kalli plunked down and grasped the edges of the seat with both hands. "Come to Kansas some day and see one for yourself." She pulled the chair in, though she could tell he was helping. *Aha!* So he was trying to put her off her guard! That was crafty! Mean and crafty!

He moved to the other side of the table and took his seat. In order to keep from watching him, she glanced around the room. The architectural details were intact, thank heaven. Most of the transgressions were cosmetic and could be fixed with elbow grease, paint and wallpaper. Lots of window allowed her to see lots of fog. "Nice sunroom," she said. "Except there's no sun." She had an unruly brain wave and went with it. "I thought you were the man who kept his promises."

He'd been placing a napkin in his lap when she spoke. He lifted his gaze, the effect of those penetrating, smoky eyes was so stirring it frightened her. "You're glib this morning." His jaw muscles worked for a heartbeat before he went on, "I trust you slept well?"

"Like a baby," she lied, forcing a smile. Taking up her own napkin, she spread it in her lap, with the fleeting thought the square of fine linen was probably worth more than her jeans.

She heard the clank of silverware and peeked at him. He took a bite of strawberry, his attention focused on a folded newspaper beside his plate. He spread it so he could see the upper section of the front page, making it abundantly clear he planned to ignore her. So that's why he came to breakfast on time. So he could treat her with utter disregard. She knew it had to be something insulting.

Promising herself not to let him detect that his slight bothered her, Kalli hefted her spoon. She ate the fruit in the silence of the sunroom veiled in gray. Somewhere out in the world, people walked in sunshine, worshiping it or cursing it. Back in Kansas, farmers stood in soy and wheat fields wiping their sunburned brows with colorful kerchiefs, and ranchers rode the range, checking cattle and looking to a bright, clear sky for rain.

But here in Nikolos Varos's home, no sunlight penetrated. All the warmth was machine-made. She eyed him covertly as she bit into the sweet melon. Niko lounged there like an indolent lion. As he read, his eyelids lolled at half-mast, giving him an enigmatic, mysterious air. It was almost as though he had the power to bully her metaphysically, without even looking in her direction.

She cast off the notion. He was simply reading his newspaper. Even so, she found it difficult to keep her mind on her food, no matter how hungry she was.

Her glance drifted on its own to the man opposite her. Dressed casually in jeans and plaid flannel, shirtsleeves rolled up to his elbows, he looked ironically like a Kansas cowboy, and nothing like a financier.

His hair was mussed just enough to make him look like cuddly trouble. *Cuddly?* She recoiled at the direction her mind seemed insistent on taking. He could have been a magazine ad for—for—well, for practically anything, from the *Wall Street Journal* he was reading to the honeydew melon he ate. With some caption that read, Real Men Read The Journal, or Real Men Eat Smart.

She continued to stealthily observe him as she nibbled. The faded photograph her grandfather carried in his wallet all those years was an injustice to Niko. He'd matured quite well since he was seventeen, turning into a magnificent specimen of masculinity.

Magnificent specimen of masculinity? She heard the words rumble through her head and blanched. Kalli, you are not supposed to be gawking at the man like a smitten schoolgirl! Get your mind back on track! He detests you and he is not magnificent in any way—well, except for his looks. His attitude is far from admirable, so get any silliness about him being a magnificent specimen of *anything* out of your head.

She chewed absently, wondering what she might have done if she'd met him before that disastrous wedding day? How would he have behaved? She could only imagine what this man could do to a woman's resistance if he turned on the charm. She shook her head, trying to rid herself of the fantasy. She was way beyond needing to know that. He had no intention of charming her. His main thrust in life for the next three weeks was to make her as uncomfortable as he possibly could.

She certainly wasn't regretting her decision to call off the wedding. One day, when she did get married, she wanted it to be out of blind, crazy love, not because she'd obligingly signed on the dotted line. Just because an arranged marriage had worked for her mother, didn't mean it was right for all couples. After all, her father had been a kind, gentle icon of men. Though he'd died when she was seven, she had fond memories of Stefan Angelis. Her mother had been extremely lucky. That was all there was to it.

Kalli watched Niko turn the page, watched his eyelashes drift slightly up, then down, as he scanned the newspaper. What gorgeous eyelashes they were, thick and black as sin. She clamped her teeth together in aggravation. *So what if he is handsome to a fault,* she told herself. *His grouchy personality could stand renovating from the ground up! He's arrogant and spiteful, nothing like your father, and you were wise to reject the marriage pact!*

The butler came in and paused beside the table. ''For breakfast Cook has prepared Caramel French Toast, mushroom and cheese omelets, salmon quiche, the usual breads and rolls, coffee and juice.''

Kalli stared, stunned by the abundant menu. She didn't know whether she was supposed to eat all of it or choose. She glanced at Niko.

He continued to peruse his paper. "Just coffee, for me."

Kalli swallowed, her upbringing of "waste not want not" battling to voice the necessity that Niko eat his breakfast. Food should not go to waste. "I—uh…" She looked at the butler, hesitating. She liked a hearty breakfast, but she could never eat all that. "I'd like coffee, too," she said. "With cream, and an omelet, and orange juice…" Her pause seemed to trigger a bowing-and-leaving reaction in Belkin because he turned away. *"Wait!"* she said, then bit her lip. She didn't want to sound panic-stricken. After all, it wasn't as though she wouldn't have had a second chance to add to her breakfast order when the butler came back with coffee.

The white-haired man faced her, his expression professionally bland. "Yes, miss?"

"And—uh—a couple of those waffles?"

He nodded and turned away. It wasn't until Kalli saw the vague smirk-induced dimple on Niko's cheek, that she realized she'd looked at him. "So, I'm hungry." She raised her chin, daring him to criticize. "So what?"

He rattled his paper to straighten it. ''I didn't say anything, Miss Angelis,'' he murmured, his lips still quirked in that exasperating way.

''Breakfast is the most important meal of the day, you know.''

He watched her without responding until Belkin finished serving coffee and exited the room. ''A lot of California women your age confine themselves to coffee and twigs for breakfast.'' He gave her a scrutinizing once-over as if to suggest her appetite showed.

Okay, so she had a few pounds on the supermodels. She didn't have any desire to be a supermodel, *or* cater to Mr. Varos's idea of the perfect woman. She hardened her expression. ''I guess you should thank me for breaking our marriage deal. Now you don't have to take on my—my Midwestern *girth!*''

Had she said that out loud? Appalled, she bit her tongue. *Kalli, what was the point of reminding him about your broken pledge? Are you suicidal?*

He took up his mug and sipped, his eyes holding her hostage. When he returned the cup to the table, his attention shifted to the newspaper, but his crooked grin remained undiminished, silently taunting and brazenly arousing.

Niko scanned his paper without seeing a blasted word. When he'd run into his ex-fiancée this morning, some part of his brain had shorted out and was still not in working order. She'd been softer than he'd expected, since that boxy suit she wore yesterday hid much of her shape. But today, in those jeans and that skimpy T-shirt, slamming into him the way she had, well, there was no longer any doubt that Kalli Angelis was quite a woman, not one of those stick-figure females California seemed to breed like broken dreams.

Good Lord, he'd even offered her a hand up. That had been bizarre, considering his plot consisted of making her life miserable. So why had his hand popped out there like Sir-Freaking-Galahad?

And just now, why had he actually *complimented* her, referring to the twig-eating-skinny-obsessed females of his acquaintance? The urge had come out of nowhere and was completely at odds with his scheme. Strange, though, she'd seemed to take it as an insult, so that had been a lucky save.

He needed to get his head on straight. Reattach the loose brain-wires and get on with his revenge. It was a shame, in a way, since Kalli Angelis was proving to be a nice handful of woman. He cleared his throat and turned the page, trying to concentrate on the financial news. Kalli's womanly attributes were none of his concern. She was not his wife, not his fiancée, merely an employee who'd once jilted him. She needed to learn that willful dereliction came with a definite downside.

He'd been fascinated by her hefty breakfast order. Charmed, in fact, and hadn't been able to hide it. Luckily she'd taken his grin as sarcasm, so he left it that way. *Damn him!* Damn her and her clingy clothes! It certainly hadn't been in his plans, but his hands fairly tingled to—

''Well, well. Isn't this a lively crowd.''

Niko didn't need to look up to know his grandfather had made an appearance. He glanced over his paper. A compact man in his seventies, with a well-groomed mane of iron-gray hair and a youthful spring in his step, sauntered into the room. He wore a dark suit, muted tie and starched, white shirt, which was his habit. His long, droopy mustache lifted in a grin that created a impressive battlefield of wrinkles across his cheeks and around brown eyes, half hidden by a leaden thicket of eyebrows.

"Grandfather," Niko called with a grin. "Since when do you grace us with your presence at the breakfast table?"

The older man waved away his grandson's joke. "Since I heard our lovely little turncoat would be here," he said in his thick Greek accent. His attention focused on Kalli; he made directly for her. Niko noticed she had turned bright pink. The newcomer took her hand and kissed the knuckles. "I should be angry with you, sweet child." He straightened, still smiling beneath that walrus mustache. "However, never let it be said that Dionysus Varos would treat a lady with less than utter respect." He released her and his smile dimmed. "I'm sorry about Christos." He shook his head and extracted his worry beads from a pants pocket to finger them. "A great loss. A great loss."

"Thank you." Kalli bit her lower lip as though in troubled thought. "Didn't—didn't I see you at the funeral?" she asked. Niko noticed she slid her hands to her lap.

Dion nodded. "Briefly. I wanted to pay my respects, but under the—unfortunate circumstances…" He paused, his hedgelike eyebrows going up meaningfully. "I decided to forgo presenting myself to you until a little time had passed. The distressing shame brought upon both our families was still so fresh."

Niko lay his paper aside and sat back. Dion's softly spoken reprimand, veiled in a polite introduction, was making Kalli miserable. No matter how sympathetically couched, he made it clear she'd committed a very unpalatable crime, not only victimizing his grandson, but abusing the family honor. Niko pursed his lips, observing the pain glimmering in her eyes. He had to give his grandfather credit. The old patriarch knew how to wound with a mannerly smile.

Niko decided his ex-fiancée had suffered enough, for the moment. She needed to be kept on a tight leash, but much more of Dion's softly spoken scolding and she'd break and run.

"Grandfather, sit down." Niko waved toward a chair. "Have you given Cook your breakfast order?"

The old man made a disgusted face. "*Pah* on your American food, Pal. I've instructed Cook to prepare me a plate of figs and toast."

Niko indicated a chair. "I feel sure Cook is up to the challenge. Sit. Have some coffee." As Dion seated himself, Niko turned to Kalli. "My grandfather will be here for the duration, Miss Angelis." He took up his paper again, reprising his plan to ignore her. "He can referee."

She said something he couldn't quite hear, so he peered her way. "Excuse me?"

She scraped the bottom of her honeydew and didn't look at him. "I said, oh, goodie. He's so delightfully impartial."

Niko fought a grin and snapped his paper, attempting to feel his usual interest in stock market fluctuations.

Niko's grandfather was an unexpected problem for Kalli. His appealing smile and gentle tone didn't mask his abhorrence for her and what she'd done to his beloved grandson. As far as Dion Varos was concerned, she'd stomped all over Niko's pride and abused grandpa Chris's memory, as well. It was crystal clear that in Dion's mind, the fact that she'd backed out of the wedding was the worst kind of betrayal. Yet, he'd treated her with the greatest, old world courtesy. It was scary, a complication she hadn't expected and didn't need.

Kalli worked like a horse, avoiding Niko and his grandfather. She accomplished a lot and got filthy crawling around ripping up carpeting to check the floor, carefully peeling back dusty layers of wallpaper, measuring, climbing up and down ladders, taking hand-cramping notes.

A trillion decisions had to be made. Once photographing, documenting and recording were done, the real work began, no small part of which would be decorating choices—taking into consideration every nuance of the home, its natural lighting, its vintage and historical importance to name a few. The task was monumental and would be time-consuming. By day's end, Kalli had just begun to scrape the surface.

By seven o'clock she felt gritty and weary and in no mood to deal with Niko and his grandfather. Reminding herself she could *not* wimp out and ask for dinner in her room, she opted to ask Cook for a quick sandwich and a glass of milk, so she could gulp it down in the kitchen, go upstairs to her room, bathe and fall into bed. Surely tonight she would sleep better. She was dead tired.

The cook, a matronly woman with sturdy arms of a truck driver, and the tiny voice of a cartoon mouse, kindly whipped up a delicious roast beef sandwich. Kalli plopped down on a bench at the kitchen's oak worktable, and ate her first peaceful meal since arriving at the Varos mansion. She relaxed in the homey atmosphere and pleasant smells as the kitchen crew prepared dinner. For a few precious minutes, she was confident that a pair of smoky eyes weren't drilling into her back.

Simmering dishes filled the air with an enticing array of scents, but Kalli decided her sandwich was fine. She needed a bath and bed more than a gourmet meal, no matter how mouthwatering. Besides, if the Varos men planned to stare at her with politely accusing expressions throughout the meal, she wouldn't be able to enjoy the food, anyway.

After a relaxing bath, Kalli slipped into her terry robe and ambled out on her small balcony. The fog had burned off around noon, but had crept back around four, though now it hung higher in the air with wispy undulating fingers dipping tentatively, almost shyly, to just below roof level. The chilly air smelled fresh. Kalli inhaled, glancing down at the swimming pool in the courtyard.

She stilled, squinting into the darkness. She'd seen movement, and could swear she heard something. Splashing. Leaning over, she searched the water's surface for signs of life. The moon was obscured by fog, but as her eyes adjusted to the darkness, she became aware that someone was swimming.

She pulled her robe tighter about her in the chill. The pool must be heated. It was too cold, otherwise. The swimmer made a racing turn, and with powerful strokes ate up the distance of the Olympic-size pool.

Kalli surveyed the lone figure, fascinated to discover the sleek form was a man. A tall, powerfully built man. He skimmed along the surface, executing a perfect—and perfectly sexy—American crawl. She inhaled sharply when he completed another turn and she was made vividly aware that he wore no bathing trunks. Reflexively she stumbled away from the rail, feeling a sense of impropriety. *You aren't supposed to be spying on the man! Go inside!* she scolded inwardly.

She spun away, but before she reentered her room, another voice in her brain whispered, *Why are you running away like a thief in the night? You weren't spying! He's the one who's outside, under your window, swimming in the nude! If somebody sees him, it's his own fault!*

Pausing with her back to him, she clung for a moment to the door frame. She should go inside. "You should," she told herself. "You really should."

Almost the instant the words left her lips, she turned, tiptoed to the rail and peeked over. Drat her excellent night vision. If it were not for the fog blocking the moon, she would be able to see him almost as well as if it were midday. His long, trim body chewed up the space between the deep and shallow ends. She swallowed with difficulty at the sight of glistening sinew and muscle.

When he reached the deep end, he flipped and she bit her lip as punishment for her quick, revealing glimpse of manly anatomy. Her pulse went into high gear and her knees grew weak.

To avoid tumbling to a foolish demise on the stone patio below, she grasped the wrought-iron rail for dear life. "I'm sure the term Greek god was coined in a situation exactly like this," she mumbled, praying Nikolos Varos didn't make a habit of swimming in the nude, and thanking providence for the gift of fog.

CHAPTER FIVE

KALLI wondered if Niko knew what he was doing to her, swimming out there every night in the nude? *Every night!* No matter how late she worked or what time she took her bath, when she put on her robe and ambled by her balcony doors, she always caught a glimpse of movement in the pool. She knew exactly what—and who—caused that movement. Nikolos Varos was once again below her balcony swimming laps and brazenly showing off all manner of glorious male skin.

His behavior was despicable. If he thought he was punishing her, revealing what she'd missed by backing out of the marriage, he was not only the most contemptible, egotistical man on earth, he was deluding himself about the undeniability of his charms. Of all the colossal gall!

Not that she went out on the balcony to watch him. Not that her heart fluttered with anticipation and excitement. That certainly wasn't the case. She went out there to gaze at the quiet night, enjoy the fresh, damp air and watch undulating fingers of fog dip to explore the courtyard. Sadly for her peace of mind, the mist didn't dip far enough to mask Niko from view. Even in the dimness, he was visible, streaking through the water like Poseidon, god of the sea.

All in all, he managed to trouble her almost constantly, morning or evening, day or night, awake or asleep. While he pointedly ignored her at meals, his grandfather chatted politely and incessantly. Dion's veiled innuendoes about the ''distressing family shame'' only entered the conversation ten or twelve times at a sitting. His slights were always spoken with a smile that looked so genuine you would have thought the man was complimenting her hair or speaking of some art exhibit he'd visited and been enthralled by. If she hadn't been able to hear his words, or didn't understand both Greek and English, she might have thought Dion had a crush on her.

But since she could hear, and she spoke each language fluently, there was no mistaking she was a major disappointment to both men.

Each Varos, in his own way, was making her life miserable, and it was starting to affect her work. Her concentration was spotty and her mind wandered. More often than not the wanderings led to memories of those nighttime sojourns on her balcony to spy—er—accidentally notice Niko swimming in the nu—*pool*.

If she didn't get a break, she wasn't sure she could go on. "Don't even think that," she muttered, as she removed a switch plate from the wall of one of the upstairs bedrooms. "You will not quit! It's not like they're hitting you with sticks! Don't be a wimp. A little psychological manipulation is not going to kill you!"

She heard somebody clear his throat and had a bad feeling it wasn't the butler. As calmly as she could, she finished removing the plate. "What do you want?" she asked, sounding more annoyed than she would have liked.

"I didn't mean to interrupt your chat with the switch plate." Niko's voice grew louder with each word and Kalli feared he was approaching. "Does it talk back?"

As the last screw came out, the plate fell into her hand. Pretending nonchalance, she inspected the wiring that had been hidden behind it. "No, the switch plates don't talk back. They're better mannered than some local men I know."

"How many local men do you know?"

"Two." She turned, arranging her face to look all-business. "You're lucky, Mr. Varos. The house was rewired within the last few years. That will save you some expense." She didn't know why she bothered to report that. The man obviously had more money than California had oranges. What were a few thousand dollars, more or less, to him? Maybe her quick subject change was an unconscious defense mechanism, trying to shift the focus to business.

"I'm gratified about the wiring." He lounged against the wall with a slouchy, sexy grace that sent a thrill along her spine. She squelched it before it became an appreciative shiver as her wayward gaze roved over him. He wore gray sweats and running shoes and looked windswept, his face ruddy, as though he'd been running hard. "However," he went on, "I did have the place checked out before I bought it."

Angry that he'd managed to make her feel foolish for the millionth time, she averted her glance. "Nevertheless."

Taking up her camera she stepped away from the wall to take a picture for documentation purposes. "Did you want to see me about something?" she asked, trying to concentrate on her shot.

Though he stood at least three feet away, there was something about him that made even that distance too intimate. What was it that made him seem to take up more space than his mere physical presence?

He carried around an aura, an intensity, hypercritical and erotic all at once—the effect made her skittish and light-headed and spiked her pulse rate. She felt like she'd guzzled two pots of coffee on an empty stomach. Bending to retrieve the faceplate, she fumbled and dropped it. Picked it up. Fumbled and dropped it, again. Gritting her teeth, she laid aside the camera and lifted the uncooperative plate with both hands.

"I didn't want to discuss anything in particular," he said. "I was just passing by."

She doubted that. "You were jogging through the hallways?"

"Not quite." He crossed his arms and grinned that one-dimple grin that was so sexy and troubling. "By the sea."

She frowned, confused. "What sea?"

His grin kicked up a notch, a bad sign. "I gather in school you weren't very good at geography?"

Still clutching the faceplate, she crossed her arms. "I know the ocean out here is the Pacific, but aren't we too far inland for you to be jogging beside it?"

He shook his head. "Maybe instead of merely looking *at* windows you should try looking through one once in awhile." He indicated the Victorian bay at her back. "That one for instance."

She frowned. Was he saying she was so engrossed in her work she couldn't see the world around her? That she was so involved in trivialities she couldn't see the big picture? That was *not* true. If there was anything or anyone to blame for her mental absences, it was Niko Varos and his vindictive game of cat and mouse. He was the one driving her to distraction, not obsessiveness over her work. With a huffy exhale, she spun away and marched to the window.

Her gaze skimmed across the colorful, formal gardens, over a blossoming lavender hedge and shady stone wall to an undulating meadow punctuated with oak, pine and cedar trees. Beyond that, Kalli was startled to see blue water glinting in afternoon sunshine. The bright azure panorama stretched on and on, forever.

"Oh..." She turned to face him. "This is oceanfront property?" She was surprised she hadn't picked up on that from her research on the mansion. Of course, her interest had been in the structure, its antiquity and architecture, not the grounds or approximate location to large bodies of water.

He pushed away from the wall. "There's no beach. But yes, it's oceanfront. I like to run along the cliffs. It's a great view. So you see, there's more water here than just the pool."

At the mention of the swimming pool, she experienced a rush of guilty adrenaline and dropped her gaze. Her body prickled with re-action, and in her mind's eye she recalled another great view, but it had more to do with a contrary male than with the Pacific Ocean. "You exercise a lot," she muttered under her breath.

"What?"

She closed her eyes, wishing she hadn't blurted that out loud. "Uh—I said..." Admitting she'd ogled him in the nude—*every night*—would have been about the dumbest thing she could do, so she shook her head and lied, "I said, I hadn't noticed—a pool." She tried to look completely blank, but it was hard. Lying didn't come easily for her, even lies that were absolutely essential.

His expression was unreadable, and that bothered Kalli. He could have been annoyed or amused or just bored. She couldn't tell if he believed her or if he even cared that she watched him swim naked. What an exasperating man!

"You should take a closer look at the ocean." He slipped his hands in his pockets. "Living in Kansas, I wouldn't think you'd get many chance to enjoy a vista like that."

That remark stung and her guilty adrenaline surge turned into a surge of annoyance. "The

Pacific is not the only stimulating vista in the world.'' She bit her lip. That came out sounding strangely risqué. She shook off her unease. *Don't be silly, Kalli,* she scolded inwardly. *It's just your guilt talking. You didn't say a single, incriminating thing. Besides, who does he think you are, a half-witted urchin who's spent your poor, deprived life mucking out barns?*

Pain in her palm made her look down to discover she clutched the switch plate so tightly it dug into her flesh.

''I've been to Florida. Twice,'' she said, jutting her chin. ''I feel fairly sure the Atlantic Ocean isn't all that monumentally different from the Pacific.''

She eyed him sharply for a second before heading back to where she'd removed the switch plate from the wall. ''I have work to do. Gazing at oceans is not part of the job description.'' She passed him a hard stare. ''I'm not here on a vacation, and I don't intend to dawdle any longer in your home than my duties require. But I promise, if I should stumble across *anything* enjoyable during my stay here, it will be through no fault of yours.''

Her outburst had no outward effect on him. His smile remained nothing more than the slight upward twist of one side of his mouth, but she sensed his elation at having gotten her goat, again. Why couldn't she keep her poise around him? She'd dealt with difficult clients before and she'd remained the epitome of tact. What was it about Nikolos Varos that drove her over the edge?

"Through no fault of mine," he repeated. "I'm glad we're in agreement." His sarcasm cut through her angry musing. "If you'll excuse me, Miss Angelis, I'll go change for dinner." With a slight, mocking nod, he turned away.

She had a quick, rash thought that she knew she was crazy to say aloud. But he made her so furious she didn't give a flip. "Mr. Varos?"

He halted at the door and shifted to look back. "Yes?"

"My mother's alone now that Grandpa Chris is gone. Since she cared for him for years, she's feeling a little lost. I would like her to come out here while I'm working," she said, stiffly. "I know it's unorthodox. I'm even fairly sure what you'll say, but hear me out.

My mama and your grandfather have met. They have mutual friends in Greece. A stay in an oceanside mansion, and becoming reacquainted with Dion, chatting about old friends and family in Crooked Foot would lift her spirits.''

Kalli didn't add that her mother's presence would even the odds in the war between the Varoses and the Angelises. If there was one thing she could count on, it was her mother's uncompromising support. She stared, her emotions roiling, her expression grim, not even hoping for a positive answer. She was so mad, his refusal would only add welcome fuel to her blazing animosity.

He regarded her speculatively for a long, tense moment. For the first time, Kalli thought she could hear the surf pounding against the cliffs. Or was it her heartbeat thudding in her ears?

There was something lazily seductive about Niko as he stood there, which she was sure was completely uncalculated. Anything about this man that suggested seduction was a figment of her twisted imagination, or rampant female hormones reacting to a sexy male—

who made no bones about the fact that he loathed her. Niko Varos was not transmitting ''I want you in my bed'' messages to *her*. She steeled herself against such obvious stupidity.

''Your mother is welcome, naturally,'' he said, before turning and exiting the room.

She started to protest. With her mouth open and *You insensitive pig* on the tip of her tongue, her brain belatedly absorbed what he'd said.

Your mother is welcome, naturally.

''She—is?'' Kalli whispered, baffled by this unexpected good fortune.

Stunned, she twisted toward the wall. Replacing the faceplate was tough, considering how badly her fingers shook. ''My mother is welcome, naturally?'' Worry gnawed at her insides. She didn't trust Nikolos Varos's benevolent gesture any farther than she could throw a Kansas cow. ''Okay, Mr. Vindictive,'' she muttered, ''just what depraved scheme do you have up your sleeve, now?''

Kalli could tell by her mother's voice on the phone that she was thrilled with the invitation. Charles made the arrangements and Niko paid for the ticket, which surprised Kalli and put her even more on her guard. What was all this kindness on the part of a man who would be perfectly happy to spend a leisurely afternoon watching her being drawn and quartered?

Kalli wanted badly to take some time off to meet her mother at the airport, but that would have required a big hunk out of her workday, which would only lengthen her stay under Niko's watchful distrust. So she reluctantly told Charles she would appreciate it if he could arrange to get her mother transportation to the mansion.

She checked her watch. Nearly three-thirty. The plane had arrived two hours ago, so if Charles had done his job, her mother should arrive any minute. *An ally at last!* It was hard to keep her mind on her work.

She decided to move her documentation work to the foyer, so she would know the instant her mother walked through the door. Perched high on a ladder, Kalli took pictures of a deep cornice. Years of overpainting had left it with no real detail. After photographing it, she jotted some notes. Almost everywhere in the house these wonderful old cornices would require careful stripping in order to be restored to their original, intricately carved glory.

Once the restoration had been done—well, she would give anything to linger there after the project was completed. Stay on for days and days to rejoice in every precious detail. Of course, she wouldn't, couldn't possibly. But she could dream of how beautiful this venerable old home would be, one day.

She heard the telltale click of a latch and her breath caught with anticipation. The door slowly began to open. From her lofty perch on the far side of the foyer, she stilled. Her mother, her staunch supporter, was about to come inside.

She heard a giggle. There was no doubting the light laugh had come from her mother. But giggling? Only days ago Zoe Angelis had been so grief-stricken about her beloved father-in-law's passing. Could she really be giggling like a schoolgirl? What brought on this miracle?

Another, deeper laugh mingled with the light tinkle of Zoe's, and Kalli knew immediately who made the sound, though she couldn't recall actually hearing Niko Varos laugh before. Had *he* gone to the airport to pick up her mother? Is that where he'd been all afternoon? Though her mind refused to comprehend the truth, her eyes wouldn't allow any doubt when the door swung wide.

Petite, brunette Zoe appeared on the arm of handsome, smiling, conniving Niko Varos. Zoe's quiet, oval face was flushed with laughter, her eyes seemed larger and rounder than usual, and she looked a decade younger than her forty-nine years.

"Mama?" Kalli asked, without realizing she'd spoken aloud.

Zoe's giggle trailed off as she looked around. The fitted, watermelon-colored knit dress she wore accentuated her pencil-slim stature. Kalli admired her mother's trim figure and wished she'd inherited the same svelteness instead of the more rounded proportions of the Angelis clan.

When Zoe spotted the ladder, her glance climbed it. Finally she noticed her daughter and her smile returned, though Kalli sensed a vague glint of dissatisfaction in her eyes. Disconcerted by the sensation of being reproached, she tried to shake it off. No doubt the optical illusion was due to her elevated perch.

"*Lovie!*" Zoe disengaged herself from Niko and held out her arms. "Come down off that thing and give Mama a hug."

Kalli's misgivings evaporated. Grappling with her camera and notebook, she picked her way down the ladder. "Mother," she called, as she descended. "You look wonderful." Her cheeks were pink. Her gray eyes clear and bright. She seemed in much better spirits than she had been when Kalli left home five days ago. "I hope you had a nice trip."

"Smooth. Very smooth."

Kalli jumped down, skipping the last two rungs of the ladder and hurried to hug her mother. "I'm glad." She avoided looking at Niko, but he was very near, too near. She could smell his mellow aftershave, and almost feel his heat.

When Zoe kissed her daughter's cheek, she grinned and added. "Niko is such a charming host." She let go of Kalli's arm and took Niko's hand, drawing him even closer. Kalli's skin prickled with unwanted sensitivity to him.

Around the periphery of her brain, Kalli had the impression a servant carried suitcases inside and up the stairs but her senses were too locked in on how Niko looked, smelled, his nearness, his height, his stance, his silence and his insidious eroticism, for her to be aware of much else.

"Such a good, generous young man." Zoe reached up and patted Niko's cheek with what looked like maternal affection. "We've had a nice chat. It's as if we've known each other for years."

She turned back to her daughter and this time Kalli couldn't mistake the tinge of reproach in her mother's eyes. "I didn't raise a foolish daughter," she said, pinching Kalli's cheek. "So, Lovie, why are you not Mrs. Varos today?" Zoe only paused for a beat before she stepped away from Kalli, who could only stand there, too stunned and horrified to respond.

"Now, Niko dear," her mother went on, smiling like a smitten teenager at the man who towered over her. "If you'll show me to my room, I think I'll take a nice long soak in the tub before dinner." She coiled her arm around

Niko's, and laced her fingers with his, adding, "I can't wait to see Dion, again. Such a delightful man, like his grandson. I know I will enjoy this visit."

Kalli stood stock-still, her breathing painful and labored as her mother and her host climbed the stairs. After a few moments, the chatter grew distant and indistinct.

So why are you not Mrs. Varos today?

The question echoed around inside Kalli's skull, harsh and condemning. What just happened? Had that familiar looking woman really been her mother, the one person she would have sworn was her unfailing ally, no matter what? The one person on earth who would take her side above all others?

Zoe Angelis was a good and devoted mother, with all the best character traits the concept implied. She would *never* fail her only child. Even when plied with the sly manipulations of a despicable brute in Prince Charming's clothing.

Would she?

An hour later, Kalli climbed down the ladder just as her mother appeared at the top of the staircase. "Mama? I thought you were soaking in a tub."

"I did. Do you want me to turn blue and shrivel up?" Zoe fairly pranced down the steps, her sneakers making hardly any sound. She'd changed into a pair of black slacks and a lightweight aqua sweater. With her dark hair pulled back in a ponytail, she looked more like Kalli's slender, petite sister than her mother. "Lovie," she said in a conspiratorial whisper, "I want to talk to you about something."

Kalli lay aside her notebook and camera, wondering at her mother's anxious expression. "Is something wrong?"

Zoe walked to her daughter and grasped both hands. "I must know what possessed you?"

Kalli was confused. "Possessed me?"

Zoe's brow knit and she leaned forward. "About Niko," she whispered.

Kalli experienced a troubling prickle along her spine. "I—I don't know what you mean, Mama."

Zoe made a face. "Lovie, when you came home and told me you'd backed out of the marriage, I said it was your affair. That I would not dictate your life." She paused, squeezing Kalli's fingers. "But, now that I've met the man, I have to doubt your sanity."

She gave her daughter an intent, skeptical stare. "What exactly is wrong with him in your opinion? Is he not good-looking enough? Not rich enough? Is he not generous enough— the man who is letting the woman who tossed him aside restore this great home? The man who paid your mother's way out here for a visit? Isn't he the same man your devoted grandfather praised to the heavens? Is all that not enough for you?" She released her daughter and made a broad gesture. "What in the world do you need in a man to make him good enough?"

Kalli knew her mother didn't use sarcasm unless she was very upset or angry. Or both. So her mocking tone set off alarm bells. "Mother, please," she whispered. "That's over and done. So what if Niko is all those things? He's one more very important thing, too."

"More?" Her mother eyed heaven. "There's more about this man I haven't listed. What could it be? Is he kind to animals? Does he dote on children?'' She shook her head at her daughter. ''What a brute!''

There was that troubling sarcasm again. Twice in one day. Her mother was extremely upset. ''Mama, when I said one more thing, I didn't mean one more *good* thing! More can mean *bad,* too!''

''Bad?'' Her mother's expression didn't change, and Kalli could tell she was dubious. ''Does he beat you?''

''No. No, of course not.''

''Does he gamble or drink to excess?''

''No—not that I know of.''

Zoe made a guttural sound of frustration and threw out her arms as though to say, *I give up!*

Kalli frowned, annoyed. ''Mama, the man has a vengeful streak. He's made my life miserable from the moment we met at the airport. So I know from personal experience he's far from the icon of perfection you want to believe.''

''Vengeful?'' Her mother's accusatory tone matched Kalli's, and her voice rose. ''Why do you think he might feel the need for vengeance? Could he have been injured by your last-minute rejection?'' she challenged. ''He's a Varos, a fine old Greek family with great family pride. What if the situation were reversed? Wouldn't you feel vengeful, too?''

''No,'' Kalli said, absolutely sure she meant it. Well, almost absolutely sure. ''No, I'd get on with my life and—and forget it.'' She had a quick thought and tossed it into the argument. ''Daddy wouldn't have behaved so badly!''

Zoe's expression changed for a moment, to sudden thoughtfulness, then the deep frown returned. ''Your father would have come after me with a meat cleaver.''

''What?'' Kalli didn't believe it. Couldn't even compute such a ridiculous statement. ''That's not funny.''

''I didn't mean it to be, Lovie. Your father had a temper. And healthy male pride. He doted on you as a father will, but he could be very angry and unforgiving when he felt wronged. Certainly he would have been vengeful, and if he were alive today, he would not be happy with you. He would say you've stained the Angelis family honor.''

Kalli was too shocked to speak. Her father would never say such a thing. He was the epitome of sweetness. "Mama, you have no right to say such awful things about Daddy."

"I was his wife. I loved him, Kalli, but he was not perfect. No man is!" Her mother grasped her hands again, squeezing hard. The contact was firm and painful as if Zoe's plan was to force sense into her wayward daughter through her skin. "You lost your father when you were little. Naturally to you he was perfect, but don't allow that childish image to be your model for men in the real world. They can be angry and they can be hurt. They are not saints and you should not expect Niko to be.

"Lovie, I want you to *crawl* to him and beg him to excuse your wedding day jitters, and take you back. If you let him get away, you are a fool. I know, I told you I wouldn't interfere in your personal life, but Kalli, the man is more than most women ever hope for— looks, brains, money, honor and loyalty."

"Honor?" Kalli jeered. "Loyalty? What are you talking about? What honor is there in vindictiveness? Who is he being loyal to when half the time he's treating me as though I were a half-witted lackey, and the other· half he growls like an angry lion?''

''Niko Varos could have any woman he wants,'' Zoe said, her tone snappish. ''Yet he was ready to honor the contract of marriage, wasn't he?''

''So what?'' Kalli realized she was shouting and lowered her voice. ''He's a traditional man who flits from country to country and doesn't have time to court a woman the usual way. He's too busy and self-centered to fall in love.''

''For your information, daughter, Grandpa Christos told me Niko hadn't seen much that is positive in marriages made in the heat of emotion. His father broke tradition to follow an American woman here to California to marry her. Niko's mother walked out on his father when Niko was a mere boy. I'm sure having his mother run off at such a tender age tainted his view on marriages made in the name of love.''

This was news to Kalli, but it didn't disprove her point. ''So, it's just like I said. His decision wasn't so much out of honor as expedience.''

''His reasons are not relevant,'' Zoe yelled, her slight Greek accent growing more pronounced as her temper flared.

''Of course they're relevant!'' Kalli couldn't believe she was having this argument with her mother. ''Keep your voice down. What if he hears?''

''If shouting is what you need to get sense pounded into your head, then I will shout!''

''But Mama—''

''Niko isn't in the house,'' Zoe cut in. ''I saw him from my window. And Dion is away, too.'' She grasped Kalli's chin. ''Even if they were listening, we're saying nothing they don't know.''

''Mother, please,'' Kalli liberated her chin from her mother's grasp and took a step back. ''Let's not fight.''

''We aren't fighting. I'm only telling you Niko is a wonderful, loyal—''

''Loyal!'' Kalli cut in with a cynical laugh. ''That's the second time you've said he's loyal. Exactly who is he being so dratted loyal to?''

''His memory of Christos, of course, and to his own grandfather's wishes. Now—'' she grasped Kalli's fingers again and squeezed ''go to Niko and beg—''

''Don't say that again, Mama! I will do no such thing!'' She yanked free. ''I'm having enough trouble with the Varos men. If you're going to give me trouble, too, then I'd appreciate it if you'd hop the first plane back to Kansas.''

''I won't!'' Zoe fisted her hands on her hips. ''I intend to stay until you do the right thing.''

''Mama, you're talking crazy. He wouldn't take me back! He hates me!''

''The man's pride is wounded. You go. You beg his forgiveness. The mending cannot start until you do that.''

Mending! Niko would sooner toss her through a window than consider marriage to her now. Kalli was so horrified by her mother's distorted vision of reality, she couldn't respond. For several explosive heartbeats she could only stare, wide-eyed, at the petite, delusional traitor with a ponytail, before she could get her body to obey any signals. When her brain finally clicked on, she spun around and slammed out the door.

It wasn't until she'd dashed down the steps, hurried along the driveway and cut through the formal gardens to a field of wildflowers that she realized Niko was out there, somewhere. She prayed she wouldn't run into him. He was the last person on earth she wanted to see.

''What's all the rush, Miss Angelis?'' came a disembodied voice from off to her left. She didn't know how the fates managed it, but they'd somehow compelled her to run straight to the last person on earth she wanted to see. Dismayed, breathless and furious—at her mother, Niko and the dratted fates—she twisted to glare at him.

He lounged against the trunk of a gnarled live oak, so well hidden in the deep shade, she could hardly make him out. But his crooked smile gleamed in the shadows. Kalli had the fleeting notion that if she'd been a rabbit and he a wolf, she'd be a dead rabbit right now.

Livid that he'd managed to turn her own mother against her with little more than a toothy grin, she pointed an accusing finger at him. *''Okay, Pal,''* she shouted, *''what did you do to her?''*

CHAPTER SIX

THE instant the accusation was out of her mouth, Kalli realized how ridiculous and hysterical she sounded. Niko said nothing for a long moment, his legs crossed at the ankle as he continued to lounge against the tree trunk. One thing did change, however. His grin died. A few seconds after that his eyes narrowed. Apparently he hadn't expected her to lash out at him for paying her mother's way to California.

Maybe she did sound a tad overwrought, but not totally without basis. Self-righteous anger surged and she wagged an accusing finger at him. ''You plied my mother with flattery and who knows what else, didn't you!''

His brow knit and he pushed away from the tree to amble toward her. She wasn't sure she wanted him to come out into the sunshine. He intimidated her enough in deep shadow. ''You're welcome, Miss Angelis,'' he said. ''I hope Zoe enjoys her visit.''

At three feet away, he halted, his smoky gaze roving over her from the tips of her dusty sneakers to her mussed, cobwebby hair. Suddenly nervous and discombobulated, she ran a hand through her disheveled locks, hoping she didn't look as grimy as she feared. She always felt at a disadvantage when she looked bad.

Who cares what he thinks? she told herself. *Straighten those shoulders and meet his stare with one of your own. You have a right to have cobwebs in your hair. You've been hanging around in undusted rafters all day. And you have a right to be angry. His suave, shifty manipulations turned your own mother against you!*

He lifted a hand and touched her cheek and she lurched away, crying out.

The violence of her retreat seemed to take him by surprise and he stilled, his hand frozen in the position it had been in when he brushed her face with his thumb.

She pressed her palm to the place he'd touched and glared at him. "What was that?"

Belatedly he lowered his hand. Meeting her glower, his lips twitched with wry cynicism. "Your cheek is smudged."

Her face went hot, and she rubbed at the spot, upset it tingled with the aftereffects of his light caress. "Well—well, that's no reason to hit me!"

His eyes widened a fraction, but otherwise his expression didn't change. Still, Kalli sensed her peppery indignation offended him.

He cleared his throat. "Don't think this hasn't been fun, Miss Angelis, but if you'll pardon me, I need to go change for my date."

She caught the word "date," yet for some reason, it didn't compute in her head. "Date?" When she heard herself repeat it out loud, the meaning suddenly came to her. She bit her lip, appalled she'd echoed the word, and in such a forlorn tone.

He shrugged dismissively and slid his hands into his jeans pockets. "I have a lot of free time on my hands, so I've decided to use it productively."

"By dating?" she asked, with a scornful laugh. Why did the revelation unsettle her? He could go on dates if he chose. It didn't matter a hill-of-beans to her. "Dating isn't exactly on the same level as finding a cure for the common cold, but if you consider it productive, then be my guest.''

A single eyebrow arched upward at her sarcasm. ''Thank you. The date couldn't proceed without your approval.'' He turned away and began to stroll toward the house.

His mockery stung. Before she knew what she was doing, she had scurried up beside him. ''Just one last thing before you go.'' She grabbed his arm to halt him, or at least slow his long-legged stride. ''You never gave me a straight answer about my mother.'' Why was she dredging this up? Why didn't she let him leave? She spent most of her time avoiding him, so why was she grasping his wrist, demanding that he stay?

''I suppose you know Mama insists I crawl to you and beg you to take me back,'' she said. ''Since you're the one who wove your spell over her and made her believe you were so dratted perfect, what do you suggest I do about that?''

He shifted to face her, his jaw muscles bunching. ''I thought you grew gentlemen by the bushel in Kansas.''

She was taken off guard by the unexpected reply, and could only stare.

"I was simply being a gentleman," he said. "And for the record, I didn't ply or flatter or weave anything around your mother. I only treated her with the respect she deserves. Not many women would care for an ailing father-in-law for years, uncomplaining. Zoe is a good woman. I like her and I admire her family loyalty. Why shouldn't I treat her with respect?" He leaned slightly forward and lowered his voice. "Just because she's your mother, would you prefer I treat her with the disrespect due you?" His eyes flashed with fury and indignation. The sight was frightening, but breathtaking.

She didn't know what to do, nod or shake her head. Her brain wasn't functioning well. All she could think about was the outrage glowing in his eyes. It was like seeing a distant fire on a raw night, longing to warm yourself in its heat—but knowing getting too close would burn.

He grasped her by her upper arms; his features held a stricken quality she'd never seen before. "Your mother didn't make me a laughingstock." His voice little more than a guttural growl, he added, "That was your doing, *my little ex.*"

The vision of a killer wolf rushed back—an angry, wounded wolf, the most dangerous kind. She grew alarmed. Was he going to pick her up and toss her off a cliff?

He stood there, tall and taut with rage. Her breathing grew ragged and her chest ached with the effort to catch her breath. The silence between them became unendurable, and her thoughts raced, scrambled, skidded, making no sense. Blood pounded in her temples in concert with the bone-crushing surf exploding against the precipice, not far enough away.

Her whole being seemed to be filled with expectation, but for what? Her approaching doom?

His gaze raked her face, then flared with a brilliant flame, both disturbing and exhilarating. Kalli couldn't move, couldn't think. The lightning flash she witnessed held her immobile, powerless to argue or resist.

With a lusty snarl, he claimed her lips, shattering her with the fierce ravishment of her mouth. His kiss was punishing and contemptuous, firm lips coercing a response she was loathe to give, but unable to deny. She had no choice but to kiss him back, her body jolted by wave upon wave of desire surging through her.

His tongue plundered her mouth, sending the pit of her stomach into wild spirals of need. Her eager, ferocious response shocked her. Digging her nails into his back she moaned and pressed her body against his, relishing the hard, male feel of him.

He moved his mouth over hers, the savage mastery of his kiss devouring and damning, leaving her lips burning. Her consciousness receded precariously then blazed more clearly than ever. She groaned, glorying in the divine agony of his intimate trespass. Experiencing a wholly alien, unwelcome rush of longing, she thrust herself against him, wanting, needing to know Niko Varos fully, no matter what the cost.

Then, with the same, stunning abruptness as it had begun, his kiss ended. Niko's intoxicating lips no longer tempted her over the brink of surrender. His arms no longer held her close. His body, his scent, his texture no longer enticed with provocative delights.

Light-headed and feeling devoid of blood and bones, Kalli shivered and swayed, cold and unsteady on her feet.

Niko's smoky gaze, narrowed and glittery, drilled into her. He started to speak, but seemed to think better of it and closed his mouth. His expression troubled, he gritted out an oath, pivoted away and stalked toward the mansion.

Once he broke eye contact, Kalli lost her capacity to stand and sank to her knees amid high grass and flowers. After an eternity of befuddled shock, she began to regain her ability to think and feel, which was sad, for the only thing she could feel was pain. Not physical pain—though her lips sizzled and felt swollen from Niko's lusty manipulation—but the pain of humiliation.

She hadn't stopped to consider that her rejection might have shamed him, even slightly. But there was no mistaking his calculated kiss had been meant to shame—eliciting her white-hot response, then rejecting her just as her surrender became disgracefully obvious.

She strangled a sob and swiped at tears, feeling wretched at the stab of guilt and weakness his kiss had buried in her heart. Unable to help herself, she lifted her afflicted gaze and watched him walk away.

"What I did to you was thoughtless," she cried. He faltered a half step, a subtle sign he'd heard her admission. He didn't openly acknowledge her, merely continued to stalk away.

"But what you did to me was..." She couldn't put what she felt into words. The memory of the breath-stealing anger in his kiss made her shiver and she wrapped her arms around her. "I think—" she cried, her voice breaking. "I think we're even."

Niko never felt so much like a rat in his life. What had possessed him out there in the field? One moment he'd been alone, annoyed, wondering why he couldn't get his mind off a woman who caused him nothing but trouble, hating the fact that something inside him seized up every time he saw her.

He knew she wore jeans and T-shirts because her work could get dirty, but did she have to fill out the blasted clothes with such agonizing perfection? She had the hourglass figure of a Marilyn Monroe, so lush and ripe it—well, it unnerved him almost beyond bearing. *Almost?* scoffed an exasperating imp in his brain.

He hadn't *almost* hauled off and kissed her! *He'd kissed her!* He'd been so furious with her, with himself for desiring her, he must have gone temporarily mad. It was ironic and frustrating, but if they didn't have the history they did, if he'd just hired her to restore his home, he would have asked her out by now. As things stood, he couldn't ask her out. Well, he could, but that hadn't been the point of bringing her here. His pride had been badly trounced, and his plan was to give her a little taste of the same indignity. He had no intention of dating her. Of course, until the instant his lips found hers, he hadn't had any intention of kissing her, either.

He winced and rubbed his eyes, trying to block out the image of her face when he'd finally managed to pull himself away. He'd tried to apologize, tried to get his stupid mouth to do something besides ravage her lips. But nothing had come. Quite possibly because some disobedient fragment of his brain wasn't sorry about the kiss. Part of him celebrated it, cheered that wayward bit of gray matter for stealing a taste.

Maybe his frustration over seeing her day after day, feeling a crazy urge to drag her into his arms and—well, maybe that was why he'd decided to start dating. Some rash defense mechanism against what was turning out to be a raging lust for the very woman he wanted to detest.

"You psychotic jerk," he muttered.

"What did you say, Niko?"

His visions of Kalli shattered and dispersed. His head snapped up with the jarring realization that he was currently *on* the date. He smiled at—what was her name again? Mary? Marie? Myra? Unfortunately he didn't much care what her name was. He stumbled around in his head for something plausible to say that would explain his muttered self-condemnation. "I asked about your steak?" he improvised. "Is it rare enough?"

She smiled at him from across the small patio table and leaned closer. "It's well-done, just the way I like it.'' Placing her elbows on the glass tabletop, she laced long, perfectly manicured fingers beneath her chin. Niko had to admit she was attractive. A willowy blonde with flawless skin, pouty, provocative lips and bedroom eyes. If his male radar functioned accurately, she was more than willing to play any sexual games he might have in mind. ''The steak's delicious,'' she added, her come-hither smile making it clear the beef wasn't the only delicious item at the table.

He flicked his glance at her plate. She'd taken all of two bites. Considering how thin she was, he sensed the tablespoonful would be the extent of her gluttony for the evening. He cut off another slice of buttery-tender fillet and inhaled, as much to bear up under the weight of this farce as to take in oxygen.

He felt bored and peculiarly short-tempered. What was wrong with him? The woman was beautiful and willing. Why was he internally pacing like a caged lion? While he chewed, he managed to sustain his courteous smile, wondering whether the simpering nymphet across the table would notice if he didn't call her by name for the rest of the evening.

Damning to Hades his nonsensical preoccupation with Kalli and her kiss, he struggled to recall who the hell he was eating dinner with. May? Margaret? Her name started with an *M*. He was almost positive about that.

"I must admit, Niko," the blonde said, "I was surprised to get your call this afternoon."

Not any more than I was to make it, he responded inwardly. He'd met her once at a friend of a friend's engagement party and she'd handed him her card. He'd found it today by accident, and just called. He'd needed to get out, be with a woman who didn't glare daggers at him. At least that's what he'd thought he needed. "I'm gratified you were free," he said, trying to mean it.

The blonde untangled her fingers from beneath her chin and reached across to touch his hand. "I'm glad you called. I was so sorry to read about your recent—well, you know."

He knew. Everybody in San Francisco knew. Niko retained his smile with difficulty. He supposed he should have realized the subject would come up. Breaking eye contact, he glanced around the courtyard of his Victorian estate. Why had he decided to bring her here, of all places, for dinner? Naturally the estate was big, and eating alone on the patio insured privacy for the couple. But why here? Had he thought cavorting with a woman right under the nose of his ex-fiancée would cause further humiliation? If that had been his thinking, he'd have to have a pretty hearty ego to believe it. She didn't even try to hide her dislike.

In his bout of temporary insanity, could he possibly have wanted to make her jealous?

Jealous? He winced at the notion. That was truly nuts. Juvenile and nuts!

"You're very wise to get on with your life," the blonde said, stroking his fingers. "Very wise."

"Thank you." Niko's restless irritability intensified, but he fought it. The night was quiet and cool, the dinner faultless. Fog rode high in the air, making the open patio seem intimate, romantic. Gas lamps and the flicker of candles gave off soft, golden light. If only he gave a flying fig about his date. "The marriage was arranged," he went on, his tone surprisingly nonchalant, considering his state of mind. "Old family traditionalism. I'd never met the woman." Kalli's face, flushed and shocked from his brutal kiss, blasted into his head, making his easygoing facade tough to maintain. "What happened was for the best."

Aggravation knotted his belly. He laced his fingers with his date's, and made a firm pledge to himself. *Whether I remember my skinny blond companion's name or not, I'll forget everything else tonight but giving her the lusty romp sparkling so brazenly in her eyes. That should wash nagging memory of Kalli's kiss out of my head.*

Kalli sat at the metal dining-room table enduring another dismal dinner that refused to go down easily. Not that there was anything wrong with the food, delicious as always. The problem was her mother and Dion, and their drawn-out discussion of her "huge mistake." They talked about her as if she wasn't even there.

Infuriated and humiliated, Kalli silently stewed, hoping she wouldn't erupt like Mount St. Helens. Were her mother and Dion deliberately trying to make her mad? Even when they lapsed into their native Greek, Kalli wasn't spared, since she understood it as well as English.

"I must say," Dion remarked, with a sad shake of his head, "Niko was rude to invite that other woman here." He placed a comforting hand on Zoe's arm. "I apologize for my grandson's…"

He appeared confused and asked the English translation for a Greek word. When Zoe paused to think about it, Kalli rolled her eyes with exasperation and answered, "Lechery." She forked a bite of salad, lowering her gaze. "The word you're groping for is lechery." She concentrated on her forkful of salad, struggling to keep visions of Niko's "lecherous" behavior with his *date* from getting past the mental barriers she'd put up to block them.

"Ah," Dion said. "Ah, yes. I apologize for Niko's *lechery*. Bringing that woman here, under Kalli's nose. The deed was more than rude. It was beastly."

"Now, now, Dion," Zoe said, sounding sympathetic. Kalli couldn't keep from glancing across the cold steel width of the table at her mother. "Niko is not at all lecherous," she said. "He's a man." She emphasized the word with a meaningful look at Kalli. "Men have needs."

Men have needs! The assertion rang painfully in Kalli's head. She couldn't believe her mother actually said that. Her fork clanked to her plate. *That's it! That's all I can stand of their little Greek Tragedy.* Not caring to have her face rubbed in Niko's "needs" she pushed up from her chair. "I'm sorry, Mama, Dion." She spoke as evenly as she could, though it was hard, considering she couldn't help gritting her teeth. "Feel free to delve into Niko's needs as deeply as you dare. But you'll have to do it without me. I've had *enough*—dinner."

She bolted from the cavernous room, ran across the foyer and up the stairs to the privacy of her chartreuse quarters. *Niko's needs, indeed!* Obviously her mother had lost her mind on the flight to California—to verbalize such a blunt, risqué statement like "Men have needs!"

It was too much! Kalli sank to her bed and covered her eyes with shaky hands. Nobody needed to tell her Grandpa Chris would be heartsick that she broke off her marriage to

Niko. And as far as Niko went, the last thing she required was a reminder of his needs. After his angry kiss that afternoon, she'd become overly sensitized to everything about him. Even before she'd sampled his kiss, her dreams had cast her in the role of Niko's lover, night after night, in the act of satisfying those needs. How she expected to get through *tonight,* with even a moment's rest, was a mystery to her. A terrifying mystery.

Maybe she really had made a huge mistake, as her mother and Dion suggested. But it wasn't the mistake they'd blathered on and on about over dinner. Her mistake had been agreeing to such old-fashioned foolishness as an arranged marriage in the first place. Okay, so Niko was handsome, wealthy, intelligent and even gentlemanly when it suited him. But he was also cruel, manipulative, vindictive and insulting. Traits no sane woman wanted in a husband.

She vaulted up from the bed and paced, hating the nervous anxiety the mere mention of his name caused her. As she tramped back and forth, her mind raging, her heart racing, she began to sense a nagging regret.

Regret? What for? What did she have to regret except agreeing to the marriage contract in the first place?

"Nothing!" she muttered, but the strange nagging feeling refused to go away.

Some dull-witted, smitten part of her brain asked, *"So how has he been cruel, manipulative, vindictive and insulting?"*

"Ha!" she scoffed, pivoting and retracing her steps across the rug. "It would take less time to list how he *hasn't* been all those things!"

She started ticking off his shortcomings. "He lured me out here with the sole aim to put me through hell. That was manipulative. He taunts me at every turn for rejecting him. He insults me by ignoring me at meals then spying on me while I work, as though he thinks I'll chicken out and run away."

Her mind skittered stubbornly to his kiss and she stumbled. Grasping the dresser, she managed to regain her balance. Leaning heavily on the bureau, she rubbed a hand across her eyes. "*That* was his most cruel and vindictive act, yet," she muttered. "His one-

and-only purpose for that kiss was to humiliate me.''

During her next bout of pacing, she chanced by the double doors that lead to her balcony. Unable to stop herself, she peered outside. She could see the patio table clearly since the gas lanterns still burned, illuminating the area with golden, flickering light. The table had been cleared, and Niko and his blonde were gone.

She swallowed several times, trying to dislodge the queer lump in her throat. "Good," she croaked. "I'm—glad." Lecherous visions assailed her mind's eye and she winced, spinning away from the window to continue her agitated pacing. *What Niko does with his date is none of my business and certainly of no interest to me, she told herself. He has every right to date. He's single, a free agent, at liberty to "interview" for a potential wife as often and thoroughly as he cares to. I have no hold over him. He's simply my client, not my fiancé.*

Even so, he'd brought his sultry lady-friend there and romanced her right under Kalli's nose. For once, she had to agree with Dion. Niko had been unjustifiably cruel.

Especially since you found out how exquisitely he kisses, chided the unruly hobgoblin skulking in her head.

"Oh, shut up!" she groused, pacing and pivoting. Pacing and pivoting.

The night dragged on. Nervous and feeling peculiarly forsaken, Kalli went to bed three times only to jump back up and pace. Her odd sense of being forsaken didn't stem entirely from her mother's defection to the other side. She knew it was stupid, but she couldn't keep her mind off Niko or the fact that he and his blonde had left the mansion hours ago. Somewhere in San Francisco he was probably *interviewing* her brains out right now.

Heaving an aggravated moan, she threw back the covers for the fourth time and lurched out of bed. Furious with herself for her demented fixation on a man who detested her, she yanked off her nightgown and grabbed her terry robe. Before she had time to think about what she was doing and how rash it was, she stood at the end of the diving board, grimly determined to drive Niko from her thoughts.

With a resolved flick of her wrist on the terry tie, the robe dropped to her feet. She executed a swan dive that was only fair, considering she'd once been on her high school's swim team. The first slap of liquid against her skin made her gasp. The pool may have been heated, but it was a far cry from a warm bath. Which was good. The cool water soothed her fiery hide as she swam back and forth in her mad, mindless race to wash visions of Niko and his woman from her head.

The water caressed her skin, and Kalli tried not to think of the sensation as a feeble substitute for what she really desired—Niko's strong, masterful hands running over her flesh, stroking, holding her close, the way he had for one brief, miraculous moment this afternoon.

''Hello, there.''

Kalli heard the deep voice just as she was about to do a racing flip to begin another frenzied lap. But Niko's hello disconcerted her so, all she could do was inhale a mouthful of water and go into a spasm of coughing and gagging. She grasped for the side and held on for dear life, choking and sputtering.

''Would you like me to help?''

She shook her head. With one eye closed, she squinted up at him.

Since someone had neglected to turn off the gas lanterns, he was all too easy to see. He knelt less than a foot from the ledge. The top button of his dress shirt was undone and his tie was gone. He'd tossed his suit jacket over a shoulder and held it with one finger, giving him a casual, princely air. His hair was devil-ishly mussed, as though he'd taken a long drive in his convertible, or more likely, his dinner-date had spent lust-filled hours trailing her fingers through the silky stuff. The effect was sexy and provocative, and Kalli wished she didn't care which scenario was correct.

When her spasm eased, she managed to suck in a shot of air.

He cocked his head as though curious. "Out for a midnight swim?"

His mocking question and half grin snapped her from her addled state. She pressed herself against the side of the pool to preserve her modesty, though she feared it was too late to hide anything he hadn't seen.

"What do you think you're doing?" she de-manded hoarsely. "How dare you spy on me while I'm—while I'm..." She couldn't bring herself to say the word.

"Naked?" he supplied with the lift of one brow.

Though the pool's temperature was barely tepid, Kalli's whole body burned. She was surprised the water around her didn't boil and give off steam. "I—I suppose you think because this is your property, you have a right to sneak around peeping at people."

He rested a forearm on his raised knee and gave her the oddest look. "Actually I thought this was payback."

Confused she glared at him. "What?"

With a nod, he indicated a shadowy area away from the light. "I was sitting over there when you came out and did your striptease on the diving board."

Her heart sank to her toes and her lips sagged open.

"I thought you were paying me back for those nights you stood on your balcony watching me swim."

There was no explaining why the water wasn't bubbling now. It had every right to. Mortified beyond words, she stared at him. Her throat ached; blood pounded in her ears. Her

body began to shake uncontrollably. "Oh—
my—Lord..." she whimpered.

"I gather that's not what you had in mind."
His taunting, coupled with his derisive grin,
were intolerable, but she couldn't seem to do
anything but stare. The image of him, sitting
in the dark, *watching* her, thinking...thinking
what? That the next step would be nude lap-
dancing?

A guttural groan escaped her throat and she
dipped her head underwater to cool her flam-
ing cheeks. When she came up for air, he was
still there, drat him!

"If you're enjoying this half as much as I
think you are," she snapped, "I swear, I'll get
even!"

His impertinent smile broadened. "No need,
Miss Angelis. I just did." After the appalling
pulse beat it took for her to absorb his gibe,
he stood. "So you'll be prepared, I plan to
swim tomorrow night." Indicating her balcony, he winked. "Don't be late."

He began to stroll away. Every step he took
added fuel to her indignation and intensified
her anger. Delirious with rage and dismay, she
shouted, "Why are you here, anyway? Did

your *productive* date turn out to be less than productive?'' Kalli bit her tongue. Where had that ridiculous query come from? Did she really want a blow-by-blow of his debauchery?

He stilled and glanced over his shoulder. His lips puckered with annoyance, but he didn't respond. Unfortunately he didn't have to. She knew, with heart-wrenching conviction, her challenge was laughable. From the glimpses Kalli had seen of the blond nymph, she'd hung all over Niko, panting and drooling, her lust revoltingly transparent.

''Good night, Miss Angelis,'' he said, his voice firm, final. Turning his back, he walked into the shadows.

CHAPTER SEVEN

NIKO never imagined he'd spend the night quite this way—crouched on the edge of his bed, doubled over with his head in his hands, cursing himself. He was beginning to regret his hasty thirst for revenge.

Picturing Kalli's face, he muttered, ''Do you have any clue what kind of damage your buff-bare display did to me?''

Damn! He'd been so bent on vengeance, he'd stifled any other feelings—until the blasted kiss. That had been troubling enough. Then tonight, when she'd dropped her robe, he'd felt like he'd been kicked in the gut with a steel-toed boot.

Reliving the moment caused another pile-driving blow to his midsection. He groaned and took up cursing himself. Tonight's blond experiment was a failure. When he drove her home, he'd found himself inexplicably wanting to drop her at her door, not his original plan by any means. But a cold discontent had flooded through him, making it imperative that he get back to the mansion.

Leaving his date on her front porch hadn't been easy. She'd hung on like a chronic cough. With no other choice, he'd resorted to calling her by the wrong name. That had taken neither skill nor luck, since practically any name he could have chosen would have been wrong. The instant he called her by the wrong name, Niko confirmed a suspicion about women. They might want you, might not take no for an answer. But call a date Maybelle when her name is Mindy, and she will instantly turn to ice.

His smile was less due to humor than weary sheepishness. He'd been a worm tonight. A rat yesterday afternoon in the field, and a worm tonight. He didn't have much further down the vile-life-form list to slide before he was a dirty germ.

''Why didn't I go with the flow?'' he mumbled, perplexed at his behavior.

Why hadn't he indulged in the sensual treats his date offered? Why did he feel punch-drunk and down for the count? What was his problem? Was this hang-up over Kalli a case of wanting what he couldn't have? The lure of forbidden fruit? If so, he'd be relieved when the ripe, little peach finished her work and went back to Kansas.

One sure thing this debacle had taught him was how messy revenge could be, hardly as satisfying as he'd expected. Talk about an ironic backlash. Out of nowhere, like lightning that rips and dazzles, he had a bad burn going for a woman he had every intention of hating.

Kalli worked like a demon, her only recourse if she intended to get her mind off the sordid swimming pool episode. But even as she worked single-mindedly, she wasn't kidding herself. Nothing, not even blunt head trauma and the glorious oblivion of amnesia would wash that living nightmare from her brain.

What had possessed her to swim in the nude? She wasn't in the habit of doing anything so wanton and rash. Just because she hadn't brought a swimsuit was no excuse. Panties and a bra would have been better than…

She closed her eyes and moaned, not a bright thing to do considering she was perched atop a ten-foot ladder, photographing the drawing-room ceiling. By some freak miracle, the previous owners hadn't painted over one of the most lavish examples of floral plaster-work she'd ever seen, though its hand-painted detail was faded and flaking with age. She thanked whatever lucky serendipity that spared the dramatic ceiling from a paint roller and several coats of banana-yellow latex.

She tried to drag her mind away from last night and the scorn glittering in Niko's fire-lit gaze. Placing her camera to her eye, she vowed she would *not* allow his tormenting to derail her. She was here to do the best darn job she had in her. She would show him she was no coward and certainly not a quitter.

Even if everyone in the house was against her, she would come through this trial and turn it into a triumph. She could almost see the article in *Architectural Digest* now. ''Nikolos Varos employed the aid of restoration expert, Kalli Angelis, who recreated one of the most authentic Victorian homes in existence today, true to that era's architecture, every aspect harking back to a cultured dignity befitting the historically significant edifice.''

With a dreamy smile, she snapped another photograph, then shifted to get her last picture. She peered through the viewfinder, focused, then frowned, taking the camera away from her face. A heavy lacing of cobweb blocked much of the shot. She stretched to whisk it away, but couldn't quite reach. "Drat," she muttered. Hooking a foot around the opposing leg of the ladder to help anchor her, she leaned further out.

As she extended her arm, stretching her body to its limits, she berated herself for not thinking to bring something to use as an extension—an ink pen, even a rolled sheet of newspaper. If she'd only remembered to grab something. "I blame Niko," she grunted out, straining for the cobweb. "If it weren't for his infernal ragging, I wouldn't be so distr-aaac—" The final word mutated into a horror-stricken shriek when she tilted a fraction too far, throwing the ladder off balance. It pitched sideways, toppling her from her perch.

Kalli's life flashed before her eyes as she plummeted. Her speedy descent ended abruptly and painlessly as the ladder hit with an ear-splitting crash. Stunned that she'd miraculously avoided the same messy fate, she opened her eyes to discover she'd landed in a pair of sturdy arms. Instinctively she grabbed, her heart flooding with gratitude for her savior. If he hadn't actually saved her life, he'd certainly spared her an assortment of broken bones.

Another millisecond ticked by before she grasped the fact that her benefactor was Niko Varos. Sadly the realization was too late to halt her spontaneous thank-you-for-saving-me kiss. When the data belatedly registered, her lips had already found his and she was in the middle of a desperate hug.

At the instant of realization, however, her eyes popped wide and she lurched away, though her arms still encircled his neck. *"Oh!"* she gasped. "I—I…" Even though the contact had been brief, her lips tingled, and his taste—moist and masculine—lingered on her mouth.

His expression was troubled. His cheek muscles stood out, too, suggesting clenched teeth. Well, what did she expect? Whoops of excitement? He'd made his feelings for her all too clear.

Her thought processes sluggishly returned to their normal settings where Niko was concerned—suspicion, annoyance and upsetting ambivalence. "What did you do?" she demanded. Snaking her hands from around his neck, she pressed them against his chest. "*Kick* the ladder?"

His eyebrows dipped further and Kalli became aware of a blood vessel pulsing in his temple. "Sure, kicking ladders is a hobby of mine," he said. "Too bad I keep forgetting to move out of the way."

His sarcasm stung, but Kalli knew she deserved it. He'd done a heroic thing. He could have been hurt. Casting her gaze to her hands plastered against his chest, she worked at swallowing her animosity and injured pride.

Her cheeks warmed, so she knew she was blushing. "Okay, okay, I apologize. That remark was uncalled-for." She sneaked a brief peek at his face. "Thank you for...what you did. I—I realize I'm no feather." That last admission came out a little cringing. She was sure she felt like a sack of wet cement. If he didn't have a ruptured disk, it would be a miracle. "Are you okay?" she asked, shamefaced.

''I'll live.'' His expression didn't ease. The blood vessel in his temple continued to throb, and his jaw muscles went on bunching. ''What the hell were you doing up there?'' he asked. ''Trying out for the Cirque de Broken Back?''

She looked away, feeling stupid. ''I was trying to brush off a cobweb so I could take a picture.''

''I see.''

He didn't put her down and didn't say anything else. The strain of being in his arms, inhaling his scent and knowing he was scowling his disapproval was taking its toll. Fidgety, Kalli ran her tongue around her lips. Another stupid move, since it intensified her capacity to savor his taste. She cleared her throat. ''You can put me down, now.''

It took him three pulse beats to respond. Kalli knew that because she couldn't seem to keep from watching the blood vessel in his temple. ''Right,'' he ground out, lowering her to the wood planks.

Kalli didn't feel well. She was dizzy and her stomach was all fluttery. Grabbing at straws, she indicated the camera hanging around her neck. "I—I'm out of film." Without further explanation or eye contact she tore out of the room.

The rapid *squeak-squeak* of Kalli's sneakers grew faint, then disappeared. Niko didn't watch her go, preferring to stare at something less inflammatory than the backside of her jeans. He scanned the room, noticing the fallen ladder had split a boomerang shaped end table down the middle, and sent flying a polished aluminum crook-neck lamp that now looked very much like a wrecked alien spaceship. Stepping around the mess, he cast his gaze over the rest of the room's streamlined furnishings, homing in on a modular chair that looked like a big spoon. It sported lime-green vinyl upholstery and was held aloft by a tripod of metal legs.

Expelling a long breath, he walked to the narrow seat and dropped into it. When he slumped back, it groaned under his weight. Lolling his head on the thinly padded rim, he stared at the ceiling. Embossed flowers and vines spiraled and twisted everywhere, like a garden gone wild. "She almost died taking pictures of *that?*" he muttered, closing his eyes.

Why did he feel so drained? He'd done nothing but sleep, eat, swim and jog for the past week. He should be well-rested and full of energy.

"What the hell am I doing in this mishmash?" he mumbled. "Lusting like a half-wit after the *same* fickle female who dumped me? Does too much leisure time drive a man insane?"

"Revenge is sweet, no?"

Niko couldn't mistake his grandfather's voice. Annoyed the old busybody had found him contemplating his own stupidity, he sat up and frowned. Dion stood in the drawing room's entrance, looking well-groomed and jolly. He wagged his bushy eyebrows. "No?"

Niko had an urge to lie and say he was delirious with the way things were moving, but for some reason he couldn't bring himself to say such crap. He blew out a breath and slumped forward, resting his forearms on his thighs. "No." He stared at the floor. "No, not very."

Dion grunted out a laugh and slapped his hands together. ''Ha! Christos and I knew you and Kalli were meant to be.''

Niko's head snapped up and he shot a damning look at his grandfather.

Dion waved off the silent reprimand. ''Bah!'' Stirring the air with broad, expressive motions, he went on. ''Pal, be wise! Swallow your pride! Go to her and propose again!''

Niko could not believe his hearing, *would* not believe his grandfather dared spout such bunk. He shook his head and stood. ''You're losing your grip, *Papou*.'' Niko's boyhood use of the Greek word for grandfather had slipped out. Obviously, he was angry with himself for allowing some odd fixation on a woman who meant nothing to him to cause him to argue with a revered family member. Resorting to Greek had been an unconscious attempt to soften it. Striding past Dion, he muttered, ''Stay out of it.''

Kalli found brief refuge in her room. She slumped on her bed, her hands so shaky she couldn't change the film in her camera. With a remorseful groan, she threw herself to the bed, grasping handfuls of the quilted, satin spread. How could she have done such a thing? How could she have kissed Niko Varos, right on the lips?

She'd been grateful that he'd caught her, true—but she hadn't *known* it was Niko.

Oh, yes you did! jeered the treacherous troll in her brain. *Who else was there with the strength to catch you? The elderly butler? Dion, who was seventy if he was a day? One of the maids? Your mother? Oh, right, like you don't outweigh her by twenty pounds!*

"Oh, shut up!" she cried through a moan. "I did not know it was Niko! I had a split second to think, and I was thinking about departing this world!"

Oh, yeah? the troll scoffed. *That wasn't a thank you kiss, little missy! That was a take-me-to-bed kiss, and you know it!*

She squeezed her eyes shut. No matter how ugly the truth, it was still the truth. She buried her face in the satin and wailed, "Oh— Lord..." Maybe she hadn't known it was Niko on a conscious level, but somewhere in her subconscious, a very guilty cluster of brain cells had some explaining to do.

Since shaming her had been Niko's one and only reason for manipulating her to take this job, he had to be tickled pink now, because he'd certainly accomplished his goal! *She'd kissed him with undisguised hunger!* How desperately humiliating.

Sniffling, she fought to get hold of herself. This pity party had to end. She couldn't let him see how humbled and disgraced her hot, impulsive kiss had made her feel. Thank heaven she'd come to her senses and it had been brief.

''Quit that!'' she commanded, determined to regain mastery over her shaking body. She had work to do. If she kept at it, she could have the basic plans for the restoration done in a week. Maybe less, if she slaved night and day. The sooner she was gone, the better for her mental health—not to mention her physical well-being. After all, she couldn't count on Niko strolling beneath the ladder the next time her harebrained absentmindedness caused her to topple.

She didn't dare risk another of his kisses. The two she'd experienced would torment her dreams for a long time to come. She might not survive a third without doing something so reckless and hot-blooded, she couldn't contemplate it without blushing.

Living the rest of her life taunted by memories of Niko's lovemaking was too much to bear, no matter how huge a bump in her career this job would generate. She knew in the deepest, womanly part of her that Niko would be a skillful lover. Knowing him intimately would forever haunt her, defeat her.

How sadly ironic, that to Niko, a night of passion between them would mean little on an emotional level. But Kalli was convinced, in his ledger of life's debits and credits, he would record the conquest of the woman who jilted him as the ultimate, sweet revenge.

Niko wasn't happy about this errand, but it was the servants' night off and Dion and Zoe were hurrying off to attend a play in San Francisco. Unfortunately no one was available to deliver the message but him. He hiked the back stairs to the third floor where Kalli had been working all day. He hadn't seen her, which had been fine with him. He needed space from the woman. It seemed like the more time he spent around her the more trouble he had fighting his attraction, and the angrier he got with her for rejecting him. He didn't like her but he couldn't get her out of his head, and he was beginning to fear for his sanity.

Inhaling for self-control, he knocked on the first bedroom door. "Miss Angelis?"

No answer. He moved down the hall and knocked at the next door. "Miss Angelis?"

Nothing. He ground out a curse and strode to the third and last door on the ocean side. *"Miss Angelis?"* he shouted, banging his fist on the solid mahogany. So much for self-control.

"What?" she called from inside. "I hope it's important, because you made me cut my knee!"

He turned the knob. The door stuck, so he had to put his shoulder to it. With a mighty shove and the creak of old hinges, he managed to get inside. The room was plainly furnished, with only a bed, small dresser and one, straight-back chair. Apparently it had been used as servant's quarters at one time, but had housed nothing more warm-blooded than dust for many years. Kalli knelt near the opposite wall beside the plain bureau, examining her knee through a slice in her jeans.

"Is it bleeding?"

She peered at him. "That's what cuts usually do." Plopping down on the wood planks, she began to tug up her pant leg.

He walked over to her and knelt. "What did you cut it on?"

She waved toward a small artist's knife that lay on the floor beneath a spot where several layers of wallpaper had been peeled back. "I was cutting off a sample." She winced as she pulled the denim up over her knee. "Your shouting and banging scared me."

When he saw what his bad temper had done, he experienced a pang of guilt, and his annoyance level slipped a notch. It wasn't a bad cut, but he hadn't meant to draw blood. "What can I do?" he asked.

"You can go away."

He ignored the petulance in her tone and tugged at his shirt, dislodging a portion of its tail. "Use this."

She eyed it with skepticism, as though deciding if it was coated with poison.

"It's clean, if that's what you're worried about."

She lifted her gaze. "I can't bleed on Armani."

"Sure you can." He pressed the white cotton against the seeping cut. "See. It's easy." He met her stricken glance. "It's not deep. A bandage should be all you'll need."

She plucked the tail from his fingers and held it away from her. "You can go. It's stopped bleeding—almost."

"Look," he said, his exasperation climbing back to overpower his determination to remain civil. "I only came up here to deliver a message." She dropped the tail, so he put it back on her cut and dabbed lightly.

"Then deliver it," she said, refusing to look at him.

After a few more dabs, he lifted the shirttail away, and was relieved to see the nipped flesh had stopped bleeding. Even so he couldn't shake his guilt and inhaled to regain his patience. "Your mother said to check your voice mail. She forgot to tell you when she got here that a Mr. Clover was going to call about a restoration project."

Kalli glanced at him, her expression perplexed. "This was suddenly so urgent you had to come up here to tell me now?"

Niko stood. "Zoe seemed to think so."

Kalli shrugged. "Okay. I'm almost done in here."

She made direct eye contact. Her look didn't leave much doubt that she was desperate to have him disappear, and that was dandy with him. He didn't want to be here any more than she wanted him to be. "I'm going out for the evening," he said, for no clearly defined reason. Before he could think of one, he found himself adding, "I trust being alone in a creaky, old house doesn't scare you."

On cue he heard a creak, as though someone had stepped on a warped board in the hallway. The slight squeak was followed by a barely audible metallic squawk. He peered at the door because the whisper of sound vaguely resembled the noise of a rusty lock being turned. Frowning, he stared at the brass knob. "Did you just hear—"

"Old, creaky houses scare me to death," she retorted, drawing his attention. Apparently she hadn't heard anything out of the ordinary.

Deciding the notion of the door locking had been silly, he shifted to see her make a face. ''That's why I'm in the business of restoring houses. I'm a masochistic nutball!''

He supposed he deserved that. Why had he made such an asinine remark? He really needed to get out of the house. Counting to ten, he slanted a grin he didn't feel. ''Congratulations.'' He checked his watch. It was nearly eight. If he planned to make the meeting with the contractor in charge of repairs on his penthouse, he'd better get moving. Then he'd go have dinner someplace, maybe hit a few clubs. See a show. Anything to distract him. ''I need to be going.''

''Another date?''

He had turned toward the door, but with her query, he looked back. Her expression would have been merely inquisitive, but for a vaguely belligerent dip of her eyebrows.

''Absolutely,'' he lied, not sure why. ''You know what they say.''

She jutted the saucy little chin that had taken up so much of his thoughts lately. ''No, I can't say that I do.'' She pushed her jeans fabric back down to cover a thoroughly disturbing leg. "What *do* they say?"

He wished he hadn't started this. Shrugging, he improvised. "Practice makes perfect."

He shifted away and twisted the doorknob. Since the door tended to stick, he yanked, but nothing happened. It was really stuck. He twisted and yanked again, with equally pathetic results.

"What are you doing?" she asked, her tone dubious, as though his inability to open the door was part of some devious plot.

He glanced her way and frowned. "The samba. What does it look like I'm doing?"

She pushed up to stand and crossed her arms. "Well, if it's the samba, it's not good." She indicated the door. "So—it's stuck?"

He turned to face her. "Way to go, Sherlock."

She glared at the knob. If deadly looks could unstick a door, Kalli's laser-beam scowl should have had the thing swinging open out of sheer terror.

"Either that or somebody locked us..." The sentence died as a ridiculous thought struck him. Shifting around, he glowered at the door. *"No way..."*

"What?" He heard her sneakers pad toward him. "No way, what?"

He closed his eyes and mouthed a raw oath. "If they did what I think they did, I'm killing them both."

"Who?" Kalli asked. "What are you babbling about?"

Standing beside him, now, Kalli stared at the door as though she expected to see whatever it was that had made him so furious.

He frowned at her. "They locked us in." He let the sentence stand on its own, since there wasn't much room for misinterpretation.

Kalli continued to stare at the door, looking perplexed for a few seconds before she absorbed his meaning. Her eyes went wide and she shot him a shocked look. If he hadn't been so angry, he might have found her horrified expression funny.

"They?" she said, her voice a whisper, as though even thinking such a terrible thing was a sin. "They—who?"

"Your mother and my grandfather," he said. "I have a bad feeling they've teamed up to throw us together."

Kalli's lips sagged open. "They wouldn't dare!"

He experienced a twinge, annoyed that her appalled attitude rankled him. "Yeah, I'm thrilled, too."

"But—but..."

He exhaled tiredly, glancing around. "There should be something in here I can use to hammer the blasted door off its hinges."

"Do what?"

She sounded so offended by his plan, he stopped and looked at her, confused. "Is there a problem?"

"I'll say there is," she said. "Nobody touches those hinges but a professional. That door is over one hundred years old. You're not going to go banging on its hardware with a shoe and a nail!"

He couldn't believe what he was hearing. "Look, it's my blasted house, if I want to bang on the hinges with a shoe and a nail...if I can unearth a cussed nail—I will."

"No. I won't allow it."

He glared at her, incredulous. "Would you prefer to spend the night in here with me?"

Her adamant expression mutated to one of fear. *Oh, fine. Fear, yet!* What did she think he would do, attack her? His mind veered to a couple of days ago, out in that damned field and he experienced a stab of remorse. Okay, so he'd grabbed her and kissed her, but that hadn't been…

He ground his teeth, cursing himself and his rashness. He wasn't usually an impetuous idiot. *Well,* he finally amended in his head, *I won't attack you—again.*

"Er—no—no, of course I don't want to spend the night here with you. But you have to think of the historical significance of the house. Even the antique hardware is invaluable in an historic sense."

Frustrated, he ran a hand through his hair. "Okay, okay." With an impatient gesture, he indicated the two windows. "How do you feel about scaling walls?"

She made a pained face. "Not good."

He crossed the room to open one of the two windows, to check out the possibilities for escape. Maybe there was a tree with a branch near enough and big enough to hold him. On a par with how the rest of the evening was proceeding, the window didn't budge, even after he'd used all the considerable strength from added adrenaline. *"Hell."*

"No luck?"

He didn't look at her as he moved to the other window. "Oh, yeah. A strained back is what I was going for."

He could hear her quick inhale and long, despondent exhale.

After several failed attempts at the other window, he muttered, "I could break the glass."

"Oh, heavens no! That's original, handmade stained glass! You break it over my dead body!"

He turned to scowl at her. "Don't tempt me."

She seemed to grow at least two inches taller as she stared daggers at him. "I just have two words for you, Mr. Varos?"

"Oh?" he asked. "Aren't there three words in 'Go to hell'?"

"Yes, and hold that thought. But there are only two in 'Shut up!'"

He didn't know why, but her pugnacious attitude tickled him. She might be fickle and disloyal, but he had to admit one thing. The girl had spunk.

"Okay, Miss Angelis, since you won't let me harm a hair on this precious historically significant room's head, I'd say we're prisoners. Is that your take on the subject?"

She pursed her lips, her gaze falling to the floor.

She was about as delighted as Anne Boleyn upon hearing she would soon have a date with a French swordsman in an executioner's mask. Niko shook his ahead. He'd never experienced reluctance from a woman faced with the imperative of spending a night in a bedroom with him. His ego was not a happy camper around Kalli Angelis.

What was it about this female that annoyed and frustrated him at every turn, leaving him constantly restless and irritable? Damn her to Hades! He'd teach her to drive him to distraction. In another minute she'd be scrambling around praying to find a nail and begging him for the use of his shoe.

Quirking a mocking grin, he asked, "Since there's only one bed, Miss Angelis, how do you feel about sleeping with me?"

CHAPTER EIGHT

SHOCKED that Niko would taunt her in such a lurid way, Kalli shot him a dark look. *How did she feel about sleeping with him, indeed!*

"That good, huh?" His grin was cynical, and she could tell he'd only asked to get a rise out of her.

"Very funny." She meant to spin disdainfully away, but for some reason her eyes insisted on lingering on him. He was an arresting sight, standing there all scrumptiously "International Male" in khaki trousers and jacket, his shirttail half in and half out. Broad shoulders filled the jacket to perfection and his slouchy-casual stance emphasized the power of his thighs and trimness of his waist.

He'd always seemed so heartless, so unbending, like a strict schoolmaster. But with the blood smeared on the rumpled bit of exposed fabric, he seemed different, more human, which was crazy, since the blood was hers.

He exhibited a lazy grace idling there, a swath of wavy hair falling across his forehead and his brow furrowed over smoky eyes. The man was proving to be troublingly complex. She detected wisps of gentleness radiating from tiny cracks in his provoking guise. The insight both aroused and unsettled her.

Belatedly she managed to turn away, and headed for the room's only chair. "Dion and Mama will be back around two. I prefer to sit and mind my own business until they arrive."

"Then we kill them, right?"

Startled by his witticism, she flicked a sideways look at him. She had to fight a smile before she could respond. Wisps of gentleness *and* humor? He certainly knew how to fight dirty. "That's how I have it figured."

His grin changed into one that held traces of real amusement. For a moment the provoking part of his persona vanished, and the sorcery of his charisma was hard to resist. Annoyed with herself, she crushed her hands together in her lap and sat stiffly, staring at the wallpaper above the bed.

He cleared his throat, which she was sorry to note was enough to compel her attention to his face.

He indicated the bed. "Get some rest. I won't attack you." He held up his hands, emphasizing his capitulation. "I spend half my life sitting—in offices, planes, even restaurants, during endless meetings." He winked. "I've learned to sleep in chairs."

The wink made her pulse rate double, so she compelled herself to turn away. "Bully for you." She crossed her legs, but the pain in her knee reminded her of her wound, so she recrossed them to put the injury on top. Fiddling with her fingers, she stared at a corner that contained nothing but the most recent incarnation of wallpaper, a rosebud design, probably twenty years old. Maybe fifteen. She tried to engross herself in concerns about the wallpaper's age. She didn't need to have visions of a more human, more sympathetic Nikolos Varos. Not here! *Not in a bedroom!*

She clasped her hands in her lap and stared down at them. From the deepest part of her soul she promised herself that her mother and Dion were going to get a good tongue-lashing when they got home. She had never felt so mortified and persecuted in her life.

Suddenly darkness engulfed her. Kalli could no longer see her hands, or anything else. She peered into the blackness, demanding, "Why did you turn off the lights?"

For a moment she heard nothing, then a low curse.

"That's helpful," she said. "Turn the lights on and quit playing games."

"I didn't turn the lights off."

"Sure, you didn't!" She frowned, irked. "Of course, you…" Her accusation died, her piqué turning to dread as another possibility hit home. "Don't tell me *they* did it!"

"Okay, I won't."

She shook her head, homicidal fantasies leaping into her brain. "Are my mother and your grandfather into their dotage or have they just lost their minds?" So filled with disbelief she could hardly form sentences, she fisted her hands in her hair. "I don't—I *can't* believe this! Do they think just because it's dark we'll—we'll…" She couldn't go on, the idea was so demented.

"Here's the plan," Niko growled. "I'll do away with the old man and you off your mother."

In the bleak stillness that followed his remark, a tumble of confused thoughts and feelings assailed her. Out of nowhere, Kalli heard a high-pitched giggle. The next instant she realized with some consternation that the sound had come from her own throat.

She didn't know what exactly struck her funny, the idiocy of the situation, the bizarre lengths to which their relatives had resorted to matchmake, or Niko's tongue-in-cheek murder plan. But she found herself chuckling. She shook her head. ''This—this is just too...'' She exploded into full-fledged laughter and slapped her thighs.

Laughing hilariously, she wiped away tears. ''I think I'm hysterical.'' She sucked in a shuddery breath. ''I must be, because this *isn't* funny!'' She cleared her throat, struggling to gather her wits and her poise. How daffy could she be, laughing like a hyena while being held prisoner in a dark room with her jilted ex-fiancé who hated her?

Niko was out there, somewhere in the darkness, chewing big, vicious chunks out of the woodwork. It was her duty to stop him, but she had the same urge to kick holes and chew plaster. Since it was clearly counter to her job as a restoration expert, she had to face the fact she was *not* one-hundred percent rational.

Her tittering began to change. The alien sound was her first clue that her laughter had turned to wheezing whimpers. She felt disoriented and baffled, hearing herself cry for no apparent reason.

Wails of frustration began to build at the back of her throat, and that horrified her. Before she could stop herself, she expelled a sob, then another, the cries so forlorn, she could hardly believe they were coming from her own lips. How could she feel such a confusing mix of emotions—betrayal, misery, fury, joy and foolish raw hunger?

Hating herself and her loss of control, she pushed up from the chair, not sure how she expected that act to help. All she knew was she needed to move. Maybe physical activity would lessen her emotional wretchedness.

She took one step, and slammed into a wall of human male. "Oh!" she cried, but that was all she could get out before Niko's arms came around her, steadying, comforting, painfully seductive. His touch had the effect of flipping a switch to Off. One moment she could stand, the next, she couldn't. She sagged in his embrace.

"Good—Lord…" he murmured, whisking her into his arms.

No matter how badly she wanted to, she couldn't fight him. Couldn't demand that he let her go and leave her alone. Dazed and quietly weeping, she allowed her head to loll against his chest. Even with all her tears, her eyes were sandy and her bones ached. She'd worked long, hard hours and slept only fitfully, if at all.

For too many days and nights, despondency had held her hostage, on the verge of breaking down. Ever since her mother's defection to "the other side," her mind had half drifted in a fuzzy, unbelieving haze. She grappled, minute by minute, to keep her heart from literally breaking with guilt, grief and shattered trust.

She felt herself being placed gently on her back on something soft, and knew Niko was depositing her on the bed. "Rest," he whispered. "Try to sleep. You've been working too hard."

She realized her arms had lifted on their own to encircle his neck, and she clung to him. She smiled tremulously, convinced he couldn't see. She had no idea why she was smiling. But for some very odd, very crazy reason, she felt close to him at this moment. They were both victims in a mischievous game of Cupid. He seemed to be handling it better than she. He was so strong, so stable and he smelled so nice.

"I'm sorry for behaving like a baby." She sniffed and laced her fingers at his nape. His soft hair tickled, and she wished she could stay this way forever. "You know, Niko," she whispered, "you're not such a bad guy in the dark." She winced once the statement tumbled from her lips. She didn't care to think where that proclamation had come from. Somewhere due south of her brain, she feared.

"Thank you," he murmured.

There was a pause, as though a rip occurred in time, gripping them in suspended animation until a cosmic repair could be made. When his lips grazed hers, Kalli wasn't shocked. Neither was she embarrassed nor distressed. Her heart did a rapid little dance of wayward delight and she met his lips with the welcoming heat of her own.

This time Niko's kiss wasn't rough and angry, or in the case of her rescue kiss, impromptu and fleeting. It lingered, gently. She loved the curve of his mouth against hers, the texture and taste of his lips, the tender strength of his hands as they slid down her back, massaging, arousing.

The woman inside her started to come alive with a passion she'd never known before. A heady, new glow engulfed her, and she moaned, her whole being hungering for his deepest, most intimate touch.

Some pitiful, fading voice in her head, shouted out one, disconcerting word, over and over—*Fool! Fool! Fool!* She fought to ignore it as their tongues flirted and teased, driving Kalli's craving to higher and hotter plateaus.

She yanked at his shirttail, pulling the remaining section loose. Delighted with her victory, she ran greedy hands over his taut belly. He was hot, male. This yummy morsel only whetted her appetite. Wanting more, she slipped her arms about him, caressing naked flesh. To feel him, to freely explore his masculine torso was a sensuous and tantalizing gift. After being tortured for what seemed like years, she could finally experience the sensory delights of the man so physically perfect the mere sight of him, swimming, had nearly driven her mad.

Kalli's common sense begged that she stop, pleaded that she remember *why* he invited her here, that his *only* goal was to humiliate and degrade her. Still, the staggering challenge of his nearness drove her relentlessly on. Moaning with need, she hugged him. Pressing herself into his hardness, she surrendered to an overpowering desire she could no longer deny.

Let him humiliate her. Let him degrade her. She was too weak to say no. He might hate her, but his sexual prowess was too powerful to resist. His kisses were like fire and honey and his caresses were heavenly. He knew where to touch, how to please, with his hands and his lips. He worked sinful magic, wove his web of seduction, even in this unlikely circumstance. She was losing herself to a man who loathed her, who taunted and jeered and criticized and confounded.

Are you that weak? her brain screamed in a last-ditch effort to save her from herself. *Are you such a mindless wimp you have no backbone at all? Why are you allowing Nikolos Varos, of all men, to compromise you, when you know his objective is vengeance? Don't you understand, he would consider a night of wild sex with you perfect retribution for walking out on his wedding? Is giving up what is most intimately yours a debt you can afford to pay—and live with yourself after tonight? Is it a debt you even owe?*

Is it a debt you even owe?

The internal question echoed in her brain. The passion-drenched side of her argued that she wasn't giving anything because she owed it, but because she wanted to give it. Still, the question lingered and jarred. *Is it a debt you even owe?*

Did Niko intend to get his revenge this way? He was a man, wasn't he? How better to retaliate? His ego had been bruised by her rejection. Of course, a romp with the woman who jilted him would salve his ego. He would feel vindicated, victorious, the damages paid in full.

Did she want to pay a debt she didn't owe—with her body?

"No!" she sobbed, pulling her arms from around him. A part of her cringed and cried out that she was being unfair, that she was going to regret not knowing Niko in the most intimate way a woman can know a man. Yet, thankfully, at long last, the intelligent part of her brain regained control, and she was finally obeying her good sense.

"*No!*" she cried again, shoving against him. She knew he would think she was a maniac, first greedily joining him in deep, passionate kisses, then screeching like a banshee and shoving him away. But she couldn't help it. Some disobedient part of her seemed determined to go against her best interests. She had to fight that inner rebellion with all her strength. If the battle made her look crazy, then that was just too bad. "Get off me, Niko! I don't owe you this!"

She heard his low, guttural moan. He stilled, his lips warm against hers, his hands, now motionless, cupped her hips. Though it all felt divine, as though his lips and hands belonged there, she wriggled out from under his weight.

"You have some nerve!" she said, her voice high-pitched and breathless.

Scrambling to the other side of the bed, she hopped off. Though it was dark, her night vision had taken over and she could see him, vaguely, a slightly darker form stretched out on the beige chenille spread.

He lay on his side, looking at her. Or his eyes might have been closed. She couldn't see that well. Flustered and shaken, she brushed at her T-shirt, upset to discover it had somehow worked its way up until her midriff was bare. "I thought you were kidding when you asked if I'd sleep with you." Drawing on anger as her safest emotion, she glared at him. "Go ahead and savor your little victory, Mr. Varos, because it will be your last. My answer is no. Once and for all, a definite, absolute *no!* Are we clear? You are *not* going to get your revenge that way!"

He didn't move or speak.

Wobbly in the knees, Kalli knew she'd better sit down, preferably someplace where his woodsy scent wouldn't play havoc on her emotions. Feigning composure, she stomped to the far side of the room where she plopped into the chair.

After a minute of strained silence, she heard the squeak of bedsprings and jerked to look at him. "What are you doing?" she shouted, then bit her lip. Why was she talking to him? The depraved beast!

He sat up, hunched on the edge of the bed and placed his head in his hands. "It should be obvious," he said, his voice gruff. "I'm savoring my victory."

Those six hours, locked in that bedroom with Kalli Angelis, had been the last straw. Niko never intended to kiss her, but she'd smiled at him and curled her arms about his neck, clinging like some seductive siren. What in blazes was he supposed to think?

His gut knotted and he groaned with renewed craving. Unaccustomed to feeling out of control, he was afraid he was going crazy. He'd had no plans to kiss her, and certainly none to make love to her. But...

Agitated, he ran both hands through his hair. He'd always been able to take women or leave them. But this woman—a woman he had every intention of leaving alone—he kept finding himself taking—*wanting*…

He cursed and slammed his suitcase closed. He'd had enough vengeance for one lifetime. Snapping the latches, he grabbed the bag off his bed. ''Time to get back to work,'' he growled. Work was dollars and cents, black and white. Work was figures in straight, sane columns. He could understand figures. They added up. They didn't make him nuts.

''As far as I'm concerned, Miss Angelis,'' he muttered, ''the honeymoon is over.''

He bounded down the central steps two at a time and hit the foyer as the butler answered the door. Niko didn't pay much heed, since his only thought was to vacate the premises post haste.

He heard female voices coming from the rear of the foyer and knew Kalli and her mother had finished breakfast. From the sound, Kalli had forgiven her mother, which was more than Niko could say for his grandfather. He would never forget the old man's jolly expression when he'd seen Niko's disheveled appearance. It was enough to make Niko want to toss his grandfather through one of Kalli's precious stained glass windows. But he'd resisted, barely. That was another good thing about his decision to leave. After a month away, maybe, just maybe, he could forgive Dion's childish manipulations.

"Well, if it isn't Mr. Newlywed!"

Niko's head snapped up at the sound of the unexpected voice. "Good grief," he said with a slow grin. Niko's mentor and friend, Landon Morse stood in the doorway along with another, younger man. The other visitor, taller than Landon, was Niko's old college roommate.

"Reece! Reece Webley," he said, stunned. "And Landon! Am I seeing things?" He dropped his suitcase and strode to the door, clapping both men on the shoulders.

He faced the older man. Landon stood a head shorter than Niko. He was small-boned, in his fifties, with smooth, olive skin and a kindly mouth. His thick, black hair was sprinkled with gray; his dark blue suit and striped tie, a uniform of lifelong conservatism.

"I thought you were in Tokyo, Lan."

Niko turned to his college buddy, clad in creased stonewashed jeans, Roper boots, tan

Stetson and red Western shirt. He always looked more like a rodeo rider than a financial consultant. ''Reece, you cowpuncher. The last I heard you were wheeling and dealing in Paris.''

''Us Texas types pronounce that Pair-ee, like prairie, but you lose the *R,* ol' fella.'' He laughed. ''When am I gonna teach you proper English?''

''Yeah, well, maybe later.'' Niko looked from one man to the other. ''So what brings you two out here?''

Landon chuckled. ''It sounds to me like Nik's mind has been—shall we say—elsewhere? I think I've been forgotten.''

''What do you mean?'' Niko asked.

''You invited Lan here, fella, since he couldn't make the wedding.'' Reece gave Niko a close, mirthful look. ''Since I couldn't get back to the States for the knot-tying, either, you said I was welcome anytime. What's the matter, too much honeymoon fun to remember your dull, old friends were dropping by?''

Reece was almost as tall as Niko, built more like a football fullback than a financial consultant. He had thick tawny-gold hair and granitelike face that softened when he grinned, which was most of the time. His sunny, puppy dog manner, slow Texas drawl and athletic good looks made him a babe magnet. Niko had always liked Reece's care-free manner. The fact that they'd both gone into the fast-paced world of high finance and become vastly successful made their bond of friendship even closer.

Reece punched Niko's arm. "Landon and I ran into each other at the airport and decided to come on out together, catch up on old times. Kill two birds and all that."

It was coming back to Niko. He'd completely forgotten the plans for Landon's visit had been fixed several months ago. And he had given Reece a blanket invitation. Knowing the man's spontaneous ways, a set date would never work.

"Right. Well..." Niko indicated that they come in out of the morning fog, and closed the door behind them. "It's great to see you." He tried to hold onto his smile. Unfortunately the timing couldn't have been worse.

Reece jabbed Niko in the ribs. "So, this is the lovely Mrs. Kalli Varos, I reckon?"

Niko glanced in the direction Reece indicated, having forgotten for a moment the Angelis women were there. "Right." He winced. Where was his mind? He shook his head. Clearly the news that he'd been left at the altar hadn't reached them. "I mean—"

"Well, I won't be first to kiss the bride," Reece broke in, heading over to Kalli, "but like my old pappy always said, better late than never." He prodded his Stetson back off his forehead with a thumb, then cupped Kalli's face between his big hands. Swooping down like a chicken hawk, he planted a Texas-size smooch on her lips. It lasted way too long, as far as Niko was concerned.

"What I meant to say was, no," Niko said. "The wedding was called off."

Reece came up for air and though his back was to Niko, it was evident he was grinning. "Hot dog! I gotta say I'm green with envy, Nik ol' fella."

Niko cleared his throat.

"I think you missed something important, Reece," Landon said in his soft-spoken way.

"Huh?" Reece turned, but didn't remove his hands from Kalli's face. "From where I stand I didn't miss a thing.'' He winked, and for the first time in Niko's life he felt the urge to haul off and plaster his cocky friend in his shiny, white teeth.

Kalli took the initiative and stepped back from Reece's touch.

''Niko just told us they aren't married,'' Landon said, his perplexed glance sliding from Kalli, who was blushing furiously, to Niko, who couldn't seem to unclamp his jaws.

''Yeah, right,'' Reece said with a laugh.

''No, it's true,'' Zoe put in, her tone and expression disgruntled. ''My daughter backed out, silly child that she is.''

Niko's attention shot to Kalli, whose blush had deepened. ''If you'll excuse me,'' she said quietly. ''I need to get to work.'' With a brief glance and tentative smile at Niko's friends, she nodded. ''It was nice to meet you—both.''

She scurried up the stairs, all eyes following her retreat.

''What in tarnation?'' Reece asked, breaking the awkward silence. He peered at Niko as though he'd lost his mind. ''What did you do to her, you old cow thief?''

Niko didn't need this. Not today! He pursed his lips and counted to ten.

"You're Kalli's mother?" Landon asked moving across the foyer. "I can hardly believe it. You don't look old enough."

Zoe's perturbed expression eased. First with the widening of her eyes, and then with a slow, embarrassed smile. "Why—why, thank you. Yes, I'm Zoe Angelis."

"I'm Landon Morse." He held out a hand. "You and Mr. Angelis must be very proud. You have a beautiful daughter."

Zoe accepted his fingers. "Thank you, again." She paused, her smile fading. "I'm a widow, Mr. Morse, but I know Kalli's father would be very proud of her." Her brow knitted slightly. "For most things."

Landon placed his other hand on top of Zoe's. "That brash young rascal who kissed your daughter is Reece Webley. We're old friends and business associates of Nik's."

Zoe glanced at Niko and beamed. "How nice. Niko is such a charming boy. I had no doubt he would have charming friends." Zoe waved toward the back of the house. "There's fresh coffee in the sunroom. Would you care for some?''

''I'd be delighted, Mrs. Angelis.''

Zoe's girlish titter filled the air as they left the room. ''Please, Mr. Morse. Call me Zoe.''

''I'm Landon to my friends,'' he said. ''You must fill me in on all the news, Zoe. From what I just saw and heard, there has to be a lot.''

As the two disappeared, Niko shifted his jaw from left to right, uneasy. He could feel Reece's dubious scrutiny, so he glared at his friend. ''What?''

''I asked you what you did to that gorgeous filly?''

Reece's assumption that Niko had offended or traumatized Kalli in some way, annoyed the fire out of him. ''I showed up.'' His words held the hard edge of impatience. ''That was enough.''

It took Reece nearly half a minute to assimilate that. He shook his head. ''You're joking.''

''Yeah, I'm joking. The subject is one guffaw after another for me.'' He scowled. ''See me laughing?''

Reece blinked, looking puzzled. "You mean she just decided she didn't want to get married?"

"She didn't want an arranged marriage with somebody she'd never met."

Reece crossed his arms, seeming to contemplate that. "Oh. So she's here getting to know you?"

"No, she's here to restore this place."

Reece's confused frown deepened. "Let me get this straight," he said, walking over to confront his friend. "She decides she doesn't want to marry you, so you give her a job?"

"I guess you could put it that way."

Reece stared at his friend, an incredulous grin forming on his lips. "So, she figured out tall, dark and ruthless wasn't for her, huh?"

Niko eyed the ceiling. "Remind me not to ask you to deliver my eulogy."

Reece glanced toward the staircase where Kalli had disappeared. "Seriously, you're saying it didn't bother you, her backing out?"

Niko pursed his lips for a beat. When his friend turned back, he allowed the arching of one brow to be his answer.

"Okay, so it chapped your hide a little, but I mean emotionally? You didn't care for her?"

"I didn't know the woman. We'd never met."

Reece made a contemplative face. "I see." He indicated the stairs. "Then, it really is all business?"

"Absolutely," Niko said curtly.

"Hmm." Reece continued to scrutinize the stairs.

After an exasperating minute observing his friend eye the staircase as though he was thinking of trekking off after the pretty, available Kalli Angelis, Niko muttered, "What's on your mind?"

Reece turned back. "Say, Nik ol' fella," he clasped his hands behind him and rocked up on his boot heels. "Since this isn't your honeymoon after all, and since Lan and I were just saying how much we'd like a good ol' visit with our buddy, Nik, I was thinking, would you mind if we stayed over a couple of days?" He wagged his brows. "You know, to catch up?"

Niko peered at his toppled suitcase. He'd almost made a clean escape. And he still could.

He looked at Reece again. It had been years since he and his school buddy had visited for more than a quick phone call. Reece made him laugh. He needed a laugh. And Landon was like a father to him. Which was more important, to be rid of the quagmire of emotions Kalli caused him, or to reconnect with long-time friends who'd come out of their way to wish him well?

He inhaled, worn-out and soul-weary, not sure his thinking processes were as sharp as they should be. ''I can't—'' He shook his head. ''I can't think of anything I'd rather do,'' he said, at last.

Why shouldn't he visit old friends in his own space? Kalli had no more intention of lingering in the same room with him than he had of acting like the jackass he'd been last night. ''Sure,'' he said with a grin that was almost real. ''While we have coffee, I'll have rooms prepared.''

''Great.'' Reece slung an arm around Niko's shoulders. ''And, say, ol' fella, am I straight on the fact that your relationship with Kalli is *strictly* business?''

"Strictly," he said, wondering why he suddenly had a bad feeling.

"Good, good."

Niko peered at his friend. "Why?"

"Oh…" Reece grinned that puppy dog grin and drawled, "I'm thinkin' since you're not Mr. Right, maybe the pretty filly's tastes run more to tall, blond and cuddly."

Niko frowned. "Since I'm not her Mr. Right, you're making plans to be Mr. Right Now?" For some reason the question left a bad taste.

"Mr. Right Now, for the time being. Sure. There were real sparks when we kissed. And if this ol' Texas boy ain't mistaken, I think they were mutual. So, since it's no problem for you, I plan to give that little stunner a tumble." Reece laughed. "Who knows, true love could sprout. Stranger things have happened and all that."

Niko glanced away. Reece's impetuous nature had always amused him. They were two very different types of people, which probably one reason they'd become fast friends. Both were successful in business in their own, distinct styles. Right now, however,

Niko had lost a lot of enthusiasm for Reece's impulsive side. He even found himself annoyed with his old friend, and he had no idea why.

"Yep, stranger things have happened," Reece repeated more to himself than Niko, as though he was already running seduction scenarios through his head.

"I come here to wish you a happy marriage, and wham-bam fate knocks me upside the head." Reece slapped Niko's back with gusto. "Who knows? I might end up *marrying* your luscious ex." He chuckled and shook his head. "Life's funny, ain't it?"

Niko shot his friend a sullen look. "Yeah," he muttered. "Damn near hilarious."

CHAPTER NINE

KALLI'S well-intentioned plan to get her work done as swiftly as possible was being badly hampered. Every time she looked up from her notebook or peered through her camera lens, she saw Reece. He hung around constantly, grinning like an overgrown, lovesick school-boy. It was freaky.

The tall Texan was good-looking to a fault, if good looks could be faulted. He had a movie star face and a professional football player's physique. Hardly anything to complain about. Plus, he had a pleasant, down-home disposition, reminding her of her Kansas rancher friends. But she didn't need an ardent suitor right now, which was apparently what Reece intended to be.

Frustrated, she sighed and perched on the edge of her bed. She'd only finished about half the work she'd planned to do today. Reece's continual interruptions had seen to that. She didn't want to be rude, since it was obvious his intent was good-natured and honorable. He'd been a perfect gentleman, fetching for her, helping carry her camera equipment as well as the heavy fabric, paint and wallpaper samples she always dreaded lugging around.

Yes, Reece had been quite helpful. On the downside, he'd kept a running conversation going, distracting her and forcing her to redo things, sometimes three times. It was too bad she couldn't simply enjoy the attentiveness of a handsome, prosperous hunk like Reece Webley. It was a rare woman who would find such genuine consideration and interest bothersome, especially from a man with Reece's superior physical and financial attributes.

Unfortunately Kalli seemed to be one of those rare, daffy women. The sad truth was, her heart ached every time the blond man smiled at her. It was all too apparent that Reece's good buddy, Niko, had given the "all clear" as far as Kalli was concerned. Niko had turned her over to his cowboy pal with the same cavalier indifference as if she'd been a pair of old shoes.

She didn't understand why the knowledge hurt. Hadn't she already had it pounded into her through cynical remarks and constant glowering that Niko felt nothing where she was concerned, except a thirst for revenge? Why shouldn't he tell his friend she was fair game? Besides, Niko probably thought it was amusing that Reece was causing her trouble completing her work. He most likely felt the more inconvenience Reece's amorous ambushes caused, the sweeter the revenge.

Kalli experienced a surge of helplessness and covered her face to stifle a sob. "Oh, Grandpa Chris," she mumbled, her voice awash with tears, "I was such a hasty fool to back out of the marriage you and Dion wanted so badly!" She tumbled to the bed and turned her face into her pillow. "You were right. Niko would have been—" She cut herself off. What was she saying? How dare she wail about missing the chance to marry the man. He was so unimpressed by her he'd passed her over to a friend without a second's hesitation. Was she crazy, shedding tears over her rash rejection? She should be rejoicing.

So why wasn't she?

Her muffled sobs came in short, gasping bursts as she furiously pounded the mattress.

"No, Kalli," she cried. "You will not care for him. He doesn't deserve your affection. He isn't kind. He's cold and spiteful!" That bothersome little voice in her head whispered differently. Hadn't she seen tenderness in him only last night? Hadn't she sensed—

"*Shut up, you idiot!*" She moaned. "*You're worn out and you're not thinking straight. Go to sleep!*"

Kalli wouldn't have believed she could sleep at all, but she jerked awake and sat bolt upright. The world around her was pitch-dark, giving her no clue if she'd slept for five minutes or five hours. Shaky fingers grappled for her wristwatch on the bedside table. Though the luminous dial wobbled, she could still read it. "Eleven-thirty."

She groaned, sagging back. The last time she'd checked the time it had been eleven-ten. She flung an arm over her eyes, cursing herself for her inability to get her mind to give her peace for one solid hour. Even her dreams beat her up. This time it had been Grandpa Chris who'd done the battering. He'd come to her in her sleep, his gentle face drawn in disappointment. He'd asked, no demanded, why she was depriving him of his great-grandson, *"…little Stefan Christos Angelis Varos, a blessed, beautiful child, who, with our joined blood-lines, would have given the world a great and good leader."*

Distraught, she pushed up on one elbow. What was the use trying to sleep when she could expect nothing for her trouble but harassment? She threw back the covers, too restless to sleep, and yanked her terry robe from the foot of the bed. Throwing it on, she slipped into fuzzy scuffs and hurried out of her room and down the stairs. She wanted to get outside where the air was crisp and fresh. She needed to clear her head—and her heart—of Grandpa Chris's angry lament, Reece's smothering niceness, and Niko's cool disregard.

Niko had missed swimming the past couple of nights, and tonight he needed to work off some stress. Landon and Reece had finally gone to bed. For once, Niko blessed jet lag. He craved some time alone, to unwind. Having his old friends drop in had been nice, but trying not to notice Reece's heated pursuit of Kalli had been impossible. Not only that, but Landon hadn't been around that much, obviously smitten with Zoe. The two had spent hours laughing, chatting and taking long walks.

Niko muttered a curse. You'd think he was living in some kind of enchanted land where couples laid eyes on each other and were immediately catapulted into some deep, dark infatuation gorge, impossible to escape from. Though neither Landon nor Reece seemed interested in escape.

Niko's savvy, worldly friends were acting like starry-eyed nincompoops. Even after Kalli and Zoe had excused themselves, around ten, the men had done nothing but rave on about how sweet, lovely, bright, funny, beautiful and on and on and on ad nauseum about the Angelis women. They were sickening in the way they continually patted each other on the back, acting as if they'd *invented* the softer emotions.

It was one thing to see Reece all giddy, since he tended to jump into things headfirst. But Landon? He was a confirmed bachelor, set in his ways and hardly cognizant of females, except as identifying labels on financial portfolios. His flighty and fanciful soliloquies exalting "the diminutive Zoe" were almost beyond Niko's ability to cope.

Being forced to watch this amorous turn in his friends was enough to make any sane man want to bolt though the woods yowling like a rabid coyote. Niko didn't think midnight, with fog obscuring the moon, was the best time to run along rocky cliffs shouting out his aggravation. He opted to swim laps until his tension eased to something below bellowing level, or until he drowned from exhaustion.

Wearing nothing but a knee-length cotton robe, he walked out to the pool. Reflexively he glanced up to check Kalli's window. Darkness met his gaze. He shrugged. There was no reason she would be there. She had to be exhausted, having worked twelve hours today—straight through lunch and dinner. Of course, Reece had run back and forth fetching so many snacks, Niko wouldn't be surprised if she'd gained a pound.

He winced at his train of thought. He was out there to ease his tension, not increase it by visualizing the voluptuous Miss Angelis adding a pound to her delicious shape. He spit out a curse. Was he crazy? Was this blasted slice of real estate truly Cupid-infested, with too few women to go around for all the arrow-pricked men?

He decided he'd better watch Dion and the matronly housekeeper for signs of hot abandon. "Oh, great." He shoved a hand through his hair. "Now I'm getting delusional."

He began to untie his robe, then stopped and peered into the darkness beyond the diving board. He thought he heard a faint noise, though he couldn't quite make it out. Possibly a muffled cry? A muffled, human cry?

He canted his head, squinting to better see what or who might be out there. Crying. He had good night vision, so after another second or two his eyesight adjusted. Someone in white lay face down on a cushioned chaise longue.

It didn't take a rocket scientist to guess who it might be. Most of the household staff went home in the evenings, so that left only three women who spent their nights at the mansion. The housekeeper, Zoe and Kalli. Since the housekeeper was a woman of ample girth and Zoe, very petite, Niko had to conclude the weeping woman was Kalli.

"What in the..." Tightening his belt, he walked over to her, not sure what he expected to do when he got there. He wasn't in the habit of consoling wailing females. His woman clients had little to cry about, since his fiduciary consultations rarely caused any emotion but delight.

When he reached her, he knelt, still not positive what he thought he was doing. "Kalli?" he whispered, placing a comforting hand on her shoulder.

She jumped as though he'd poked her with a stick. *"Oh—my..."* she half-cried, half-whimpered, jerking to face him. "What..." She swiped at her eyes with the sleeve of her robe. "What—do you want?"

He hunkered there with absolutely no idea. "I was just—" he indicated the pool "—about to go swimming when I heard you..." The word cry seemed too unkind, considering he'd embarrassed her by letting her know he'd caught her at such a vulnerable moment. He amended with, "Out here." *How lame.* He swallowed the urge to curse himself.

She sniffed and looked around as though needing a handkerchief and wondering what might substitute. For some bizarre reason his heart went out to her. Hell if he knew why. All day she'd been pursued by one of the most eligible bachelors in the country. Most women would be in a state of euphoria.

He lifted the tail of his sash. "Here. Blow."

She eyed the cloth fretfully and sniffed again. "I bled on you last night, I refuse to blow my nose on you tonight." She swiped her sleeve across her face, mumbling, "When will I learn to carry a handkerchief?"

"What's the matter, Kalli?" he asked. He knew he would never understand women and it had never bothered him. He was no different from millions of other men. But for once, he wanted to know what caused her so much distress. "Are you sick?"

She shifted and sat up, adjusting her robe about her and curling her arms around her knees. Staring into the distance, she shook her head. "I'm not sick and nothing's wrong." She sniffled again. "Every so often, people just need a good cry."

That was the craziest thing he'd ever heard. Clearly women were a species unto themselves. "I don't," he said.

She peered at him. "I said *people*."

"What do you think I am?" he asked, annoyed and wondering why he was here.

"I don't know what you are, Mr. Varos. But I'm guessing your daddy was a calculator and your mama a block of ice."

"That's nice," he said. "I come over to see if I can help and you criticize me."

She looked away and bit her lip. She blinked several times and he sensed she was fighting tears. "I'm sorry," she murmured, though the apology was so faint and tremulous he wasn't positive she'd done anything but blow out a rattling exhale.

She cocked her head in his direction, her expression tragic. A dim sparkle moving down her cheek gave away the fact that a tear had escaped her pains to hold it back. "You're such a huge fan of criticism," she said, "I didn't think you'd mind."

The quietly uttered remark slammed his gut like a boulder. It took him a minute to rally. When he did he felt like a weasel and made a pained face. Feeling like a weasel wasn't his idea of rallying.

Reece's words from this morning came back, echoing around inside his head. *So she decided she didn't like tall, dark and ruthless...* Ruthless? He experienced a creeping unease, compelled to admit it was true. He did have the reputation of being ruthless when crossed.

Kalli's rejection had exposed him to the worst humiliation of his life, and he'd reacted according to his code. Unfortunately for his ex-fiancée, she wasn't a hard-nose business foe. She was a sensitive, creative woman who'd lost someone dear to her. She'd been grieving—was still grieving. And what had he done from the moment they'd met? He'd behaved like a vindictive weasel.

"Please, go away," she whispered.

He had a jarring thought. "Did Reece say something out of line, or do something?"

"No, certainly not," she cut in. "I just had a bad dream, and it—it upset me."

"A dream?" That surprised him. He rarely had a dream he could remember, let alone one with the power to make him weep.

She turned away. "Just—just Grandpa Chris. He was mad about—about—" Her voice cracked and she lifted a shoulder in a dismissive shrug. "Basically, no marriage, and—and no grandson. He was mad."

Niko contemplated her admission for a moment. Her anguish moved him, a unique and frustrating experience. "Look, Kalli," he said gravely. "Your grandfather was a gentle man who loved you above everything. Christos would never blame you for your decision not to go through with the wedding. You have to put that out of your head." He touched her hand. When she flinched, he withdrew, feeling like dirt. During their whole relationship, he'd treated her shabbily and with malice of forethought. How did he expect her to react?

He cleared his throat. "I don't blame you, either," he said, startled to hear such a wildly unforeseen statement come out of his mouth. Yet, after giving it a second or two to sink in, he knew it was true. That realization was not only startling, but curiously soothing. He was tired of being at odds with her. His vendetta had been far from satisfying.

On the contrary, his ranting had done nothing but make him feel like a—well, a weasel. "I was..." He frowned, not sure what he wanted to say. ''I didn't like the idea of an arranged marriage, at first,'' he said, going with his gut. ''It was a knee-jerk reaction. A pride thing. I can get my own women.'' He ran a hand through his hair and broke eye contact, unaccustomed to opening himself up this way. ''Then I saw your picture.'' He scanned her face, watching for a reaction. ''I said yes.''

She stared, hugging her knees. Another silvery shimmer slid down her cheek.

He went on slowly, feeling his way. ''My parents marriage was a so-called love match, but I don't remember anything but yelling. My mother left when I was still a kid. After that, for the rest of his life, my father never allowed me to mention her name. So much for love matches,'' he muttered. ''Living with that, I decided the old ways couldn't be worse, and might be more valid.''

Another tear skidded down her cheek but she remained mute. He had the strangest urge to take her in his arms and…

He clenched his jaws, bracing himself. She'd already made it clear how she felt about him leaping at her out of the darkness.

"I honestly don't know which is the best way to choose a life partner, Kalli," he admitted. "Evidently, for you, an arranged marriage wasn't right. You did what you had to do." He paused in thought. "As for me, I want a wife and children. Being the product of our instant gratification culture, I guess I thought an arranged marriage would be a quick fix. I was in a hurry. I wanted a family so it had to be now." He grinned without humor. "No matter how people come together, the hard truth is, relationships take time, and work. Maybe it would have made a difference if we'd met—gotten to know each other."

"Who's fault was it we didn't?" Her voice was quiet, but far from tranquil.

"Mine," he admitted. "I'm the one who canceled the meetings, refusing to allow myself..." He paused, wincing at the self-centered way he'd said that. "Rather," he amended, "refusing to allow *us* time to meet, to talk." This whole fiasco had gone according to his needs, his schedule. *Great planning, you selfish bastard!* he admonished inwardly. "So..." he went on, "it's my turn to apologize."

She blinked, but didn't respond.

"I'm sorry," he said, his low tone reserved for deadly serious things. "I've put you through hell. I regret it."

His apology hung there in the chill between them. She looked blank. *Blast!* Is that what his apologies did? Empty people? Or did she not believe him? Even worse, did she believe him and simply not care?

The atmosphere seemed as shrouded by gloom as by fog. Apologies weren't easy for Niko. He felt weary, drained. "For you, your rejection was appropriate. If you had doubts, you had to do it." He forced himself to smile. "I'll have to decide for myself what direction is right for me—if anything. How—or if—I choose a life partner is not your problem, Kalli. Don't handicap your chance for happiness worrying over my issues, or your grandfather's or anyone else's. You have your own life to live."

Time passed in ponderous silence. Niko faced the fact there was no reason to continue to kneel there like some desperate suitor. If she didn't believe he was truly sorry, or if things had gone too far for her to accept his apology, then there was nothing more he could do.

He stood and for no apparent reason, bent to brush the top of her head with a kiss. "Good night, Kalli," he murmured. "I know you'll find what you're looking for."

Kalli huddled on the lounge chair, paralyzed, exactly the way she'd been when his lips brushed her hair. Even her tears dangled precisely where they'd been at that instant. She blinked, at long last able to move. Trying to grasp what had happened, she sucked in a shuddery breath.

Had Niko, the unfeeling beast, apologized for all his jeers and slights? What had brought that on? Did he mean it, or was he one of those men who would say anything to get a woman to quit blubbering?

She managed to remove her arms from about her knees and lay back to stare at the foggy blackness. What if he really did mean what he'd said? What if he was truly sorry? She blinked again, dislodging tears. They trailed from the outer corners of her eyes and dribbled into her hair.

"He did a decent thing," she murmured, "trying to relieve me of my guilt." She chewed the inside of her cheek. "So—Niko, you can be gentle and decent…" An upsurge of regret choked her and she covered her mouth with both hands to keep the sorrowful sound from escaping.

Discovering Niko could be giving and sympathetic only made the ache in her heart more excruciating—because now she could see so clearly her rash, panicked rejection had caused her to lose a truly special man.

His whispered assurance came back to her. "I know you'll find what you're looking for." She flung herself to her face to stifle a new bout of bawling. What if she'd already found what she'd been looking for, but was too dense and skittish to accept it? What if Niko was her true love and she'd foolishly rejected him before ever knowing him—before experiencing those smoky eyes, his scent and his kisses. Or the hot, heady feel of his skin? And tonight, she'd discovered his caring side.

"What *if?*" she scoffed, fearing the truth. *"What if!"*

*   *   *

Kalli found herself laughing and it felt good. Strange but good. Had it really been two weeks since she'd first stepped inside Niko's home? During these past two days Kalli had become accustomed to Reece's constant presence. His dogged friendliness had begun to make inroads, nibbling at the edges of her sorrow. She welcomed his witticisms and found his slow Texas drawl pleasant. The sound of her laughter jarred her at first. How long had it been since she laughed?

Drat Niko Varos! First for his revenge plot and now for his civil aloofness. In the past two days he'd hardly spoken to her. And when he did, it was with a confusing, guarded courtesy. She'd seen him pass by in the hallway a time or two, but unlike before, he didn't linger, didn't turn in her direction, his lips quirking with sardonic amusement.

She must be a little crazy, because she felt hollow. Why was it that even Niko's sarcastic attention was better than this. At least then, there had been fire in his eyes, not this reserved politeness. She might as well be a complete stranger sharing an elevator ride with him.

At meals he visited amiably with the others, but his attention hardly ever strayed to her. She didn't care to ponder how she knew this. Surely she wasn't examining him as closely and constantly as her knowledge indicated.

Bone-weary and blue, she rubbed the back of her neck and struggled to improve her mood. Reece had tried so hard to keep her laughing, she owed it to him to put a smile on her face and a spring in her step. She'd show Mr. Cool-And-Civil Varos how much she cared about *whom* he paid attention to and whom he did not. She was almost finished with her work. Just two or three days more, and she would have all the calculations and information she needed.

She was finishing ahead of schedule, and she was grateful for that. Meanwhile, with Reece hanging around distracting her from thoughts of her disturbing host, her emotions were less fractured than she could have imagined. She was grateful for that, too. There was nothing like being pursued by a good-looking, charmer to lift a girl's morale.

Though Reece couldn't free her of lingering regrets, Kalli was determined to allow his attentiveness to divert her mind for as long as he was there.

Another workday done, Kalli and Reece headed to her room so he could drop off her camera and sample books. She stretched her aching muscles. ''I think I'll take a hot soak before dinner,'' she said, more to herself than to him.

''Need some company?'' he drawled. ''I'm great at scrubbing backs.''

She glanced at him and laughed. ''Down boy,'' she joked. ''That old roll-top tub isn't big enough for you, let alone you and me.''

As they entered her room, he grinned, undaunted. ''Ain't it the truth. The fixtures in this place are plenty puny,'' he said. ''Is Nik going to keep all this old stuff?''

Kalli made an admonishing face. ''How many times have I told you? Keeping this old stuff is why I'm here. Thank heaven the fifties' fans didn't trash the original bathroom fixtures. So, cowboy, to answer your question, yes. Niko is going to keep all this old stuff.''

Reece laid her equipment in neat stacks against a wall, then stood to face her. ''Yeah, well, give me a shower with about six spigots coming at me from all directions, and you got yourself a place to play.''

He winked, the act so impish all she could do was grin. ''Reece, you're awful.''

He ambled over to her. In pressed jeans, fancy boots and bright yellow shirt, the husky blond looked like a walking commercial for Bronc Rider cologne. Why, oh, why couldn't her heart pound for him the way it did whenever Niko happened by? She would give anything to have the raging hots for Reece. Though she knew nothing permanent would come of an affair with him, she was afraid it would take something that radical to distract her from her raging hots for Niko.

''What are you thinking, darlin'?'' he asked, taking her wrist.

She blinked, startled she'd gone so far astray in her mind. She shook her head. ''Nothing, I—''

Her sentence was cut short when Reece swooped down to plant a kiss on her lips. This was his second swooping kiss since they'd met. Kalli was shocked for an instant, but only an instant. She should have known this was coming. A man didn't fetch and linger and amuse, hour upon hour, if he didn't expect something in return.

His lips were soft, his kiss impassioned. His hands, once again, held her head. It was almost as though he expected her to jerk away, which of course she wouldn't do. What was a little kiss after all he'd done for her? Making her laugh, alone, these past two days was enough to grant him this token of appreciation. As a matter of fact, she'd almost kissed him a couple of times, herself, out of pure thankfulness that he'd come along when she'd needed a good laugh.

She returned his kiss, but without the passion she wished she felt. Laying her hands against his chest, she pressed lightly to let him know the kiss needed to end. He didn't respond to her gentle demand. She gave him a count of three. Just when she was about to draw out of his grasp, she heard a masculine throat-clearing.

Apparently Reece did, too, for he released her face. She turned toward the sound to discover Niko lounging against doorjamb. His arms and ankles were crossed, his eyes hooded. His flared nostrils curved like little ram's horns.

Lamplight struck him as though he were on-stage, starring in some edgy drama. Showcased in golden light, his angular features were arresting, his expression guarded. He was casually dressed in gray sweats. Even so, he managed to manipulate reality to make himself look both heart-meltingly sexy and larger than life. Kalli had to fight a willful urge to run into his arms.

"I'm sorry to intrude," he said, a tinge of sarcasm in his tone. "But I thought you should know. Cook said dinner will be at eight. The shipment of Kansas beef was late." He glanced at Kalli, one eyebrow rising significantly. "How do you like your beef, Miss Angelis?"

Kalli couldn't fathom what he meant by the subtle lift of his brow or the odd shift in tone. Did he expect her to say medium rare or perhaps blond?

She shrugged. "Cook knows. We had a chat about Kansas beef the other day."

Without even the courtesy of a reaction, Niko glanced at Reece. "I know what you like.'' He pushed away from the wall and nodded a farewell. ''See you later.''

Reece's chuckle drew her attention. ''Nik's a funny man.'' He placed a hand on her shoulder. ''I guess it's gettin' pretty obvious what I like, darlin'.'' He winked and squeezed her shoulder affectionately. ''I'd better let you get to that soak.''

He left the room and closed the door after him.

Depressed and shaky, Kalli stared down at her feet. Niko's narrowed eyes had given nothing away, yet she'd felt their sting. How could he burn all the way through to her soul with nothing more lethal than a cynical squint?

She felt guilty and she had no idea why. Didn't she have every right to let another man kiss her? His words from the other night by the pool came back for the thousandth time. *''How—or if—I choose a life partner is not your problem, Kalli.''*

Not her problem! He couldn't have made his feeling about her any clearer than that!

''I have done nothing to be ashamed of,'' she whispered tightly. ''Niko, you've made it clear you no longer want to marry me.''

The sad thing was, she wished he did.

CHAPTER TEN

Niko was rapidly losing enthusiasm about his old friends' impromptu visit. Dinnertime on the fourth day of their extended stay had arrived, but who was counting? Niko entered the large dining room to a burst of laughter. No one was looking in his direction, so his arrival didn't seem to be what amused them.

Zoe, Kalli and the three men were seated at the far end of the long, metal table, engrossed in lively conversation. Not in the mood to play the charming host, he had half a mind to turn around and leave. Lately his disposition had hovered around an urge to chew nails.

Watching Reece drool and preen for Kalli had become as irritating as a constantly baying hound. Why he insisted on witnessing the little romance was anybody's guess. Why didn't he leave? His guests would eventually discover he was gone.

"Well, well, Pal!" Dion bellowed, with a grand wave. "We were beginning to think you had given up eating."

Niko smiled politely. "It crossed my mind," he muttered.

"What?" Dion called.

"Nothing." He took his place at the head of the table where his band of guests had clustered. "Sorry, I'm late," he said, keeping a precarious hold on his courteous expression. "What was so funny as I came in?"

Chuckling, Landon squeezed the older of the Angelis women's hand. "Zoe was telling us the funniest story."

Zoe beamed. "Landon is such a good audience. It wasn't that funny."

"Yes, it was, Mrs. Angelis." Reece slung an arm around Kalli and squeezed fondly. "You and your little baby, here, are as quick as greased snakes when it comes to wit."

Kalli laughed. "Gee, thanks." She poked Reece playfully. "That's pure poetry, cowboy."

Grudgingly Niko deduced he would never hear the actual funny story, just endless accolades from the aggravatingly smitten, so he decided to change the subject. "Grandfather?" He glanced at Dion. "How was your visit with your old friend, Leiandros, and his new bride?''

The older man made a grumpy face and muttered something in Greek. Niko rarely spoke his forebear's native tongue, so he wasn't as fluent as he should be. Even so, he thought he caught the gist, and fought a wry grin. ''The nineteen-year-old bride of a seventy-seven-year-old thrice-married grandfather might be called many things, but—well, not what you said. At least, not in polite company. Remember, the majority of the people at this table understand Greek. Including the women.''

Dion's ruddy skin grew ruddier and he bowed his head. ''My apologies, dear ladies.'' He eyed his grandson and his grumpy expression returned. ''All I can say is, my old friend has lost his mind and will soon lose his fortune. If that woman had a brain, I could not detect it. The only personal feature she possessed larger than her bloated chest was her ceaseless whine. That young—young *woman* kept insisting she needed a yacht!'' Dion gestured broadly, shouting, ''No one *needs* a yacht, especially not a nineteen-year-old, spoiled—spoiled..." He scratched his head, apparently unable to come up with the appropriate English word, so he spewed out several colorful Greek substitutes.

"Let's go with 'brat.'" Niko broke in, unable to contain his amusement at his grandfather's rather colorful opinion of trophy wives. "Then the visit went well, I take it," he kidded.

"Bah!" Dion threw up his hands. "You laugh, but I warn you, there are young—young *brats* out there who would marry you only to relieve you of your wealth!"

Reece laughed. "But the entertaining way they relieve you of it, old buddy, might be fun. What better way is there for a lonely, rich old-timer to spend his cash?"

"Reece!" Kalli said, her expression teasingly reproving. "I suppose that's what you intend to do?"

He turned to her and winked. "I don't plan on being lonely."

She sat back, appearing dubiously amused.

Niko couldn't seem to look away. Hair as black as a starless night settled around her shoulders. Her full lips quirked genially; her sparkling lavender eyes complemented the dusty rose of her cheeks.

"Oh?" she asked. "And how do you intend to prevent that?"

"I figure to hog-tie me a pretty filly and hold on for life."

Kalli shook her head at him, grinning. "Knowing you and your indefatigable outlook on life, I don't doubt that for a minute."

Reece squeezed her shoulders. "Darlin' I don't know what in-de-fat-whatever you said means, but I like the way you look when you said it."

Niko squirmed, his annoyance intensifying. "Yeah, right, Reece," he cut in, sarcastically. "You graduated magna cum laude from Cal Tech and you still can't speak English."

Reece glanced at Niko, his grin crooked. "Hey, I'm from Texas, ol' buddy. In God's Country, we speak pure *Texan*. Anything over three syllables just don't get said. Ain't worth our time." He shifted back to Kalli. "As for you, sugar. I'll take that as a compliment, whatever you said."

"I'm sure you will," Kalli said, giggling. "If I said you were a bore and a clod you'd find a way to take it as a compliment, because you simply don't think in the negative.''

''Thanks, sugar,'' Reece teased. ''Now don't tell me you think that's bad.''

She shook her head and dropped her gaze to her meal of mussels in red wine. ''No.'' She picked up her fork and toyed with a sprig of parsley. ''I think being positive is an excellent trait.''

Niko took that as a direct shot and felt the stab in his gut. Why? It was true he'd behaved like an ass around her for weeks, but for the past four days he'd treated her with nothing but respect. He'd been one hundred percent positive. Hadn't he told her not to let bad dreams upset her, and that she'd find what she was looking for? That was positive. There was no reason to take what she'd said personally.

He glared at his plate and grabbed his fork. *Damn!* He needed to get back to work. This scrapped-honeymoon mess was driving him nuts. He'd never felt insecure a day in his life! He'd been as positive and secure within himself as Reece—*on the Texan's best, blasted day!* What was his problem all of a sudden? Why would he take an insignificant comment murmured to somebody else as a personal insult?

"Okay, people, I'm bored with Reece's character analysis," Landon said, drawing Niko's gaze. "There's something I can't put off any longer." He scooted back his chair and stood, turning to gaze down at Zoe. Niko had the sneaking suspicion a big shoe was about to drop.

Landon took Zoe's fingers in his and knelt before her. "Coming on the heels of that bratty wife discussion, I assure you I'm no lonely, old rich guy looking for a—an entertaining way to lose my fortune." His smile was so lovesick Niko felt a prick of compassion. "I've been contented as a bachelor," Landon went on. "At least I thought I was. But the instant I met you, Zoe, my world changed, and I realized how empty my life has been up until now."

He paused, his features flushed, earnest, a prisoner of hope. Niko had never seen such passion in his analytical friend before. The sedate, financial guru looked like a starry-eyed adolescent. Fascinated, Niko watched as Landon continued, "We haven't known each other long, but, Zoe,'' he stopped, his smile tremulous as he inhaled. ''I love you and I'm asking you to do me the honor of marrying me. I've never wanted anything more in my life— or felt anything more deeply.''

The room had grown still. Niko couldn't see Zoe's face, for she sat at his right, with Landon to her right, so her back was to him. He had no idea whether she stared in shock or smiled, tears of joy streaming down her face. His only choice was to look at Kalli. Being Zoe's daughter she would surely mirror her mother's reaction.

Niko watched Kalli's face. Such a pretty face. At this moment her eyes were very big, her soft, taunting lips parted in surprise. Her cheeks grew pink as he watched, and her eyes began to glimmer. After another few ticks of the clock a tear fell and she smiled.

Zoe let out a high-pitched squeal, pulling Landon to his feet. ''Oh—oh, yes, Landon!'' She hugged him hard.

Zoe's childlike exuberance intrigued Niko. She seemed younger than her daughter. He found himself glancing at Kalli again. She still smiled, and a few tears escaped her eyes, but she sat quietly, a much more self-contained person than her mother. Except, when she had a bad dream.

''How wonderful, Mama,'' Kalli whispered, though Niko sensed she was not wholly delighted. He had a feeling she was battling little-girl loyalties to a daddy she'd long ago placed on a pedestal, her ideal for all men. Kalli might believe Landon was a good person, but he could never stand up to memories of her perfect father. Still Niko had to give her credit. Her mother's happiness was important to her, too, so her negative thoughts would never be voiced.

He had an odd notion. Maybe those negative thoughts should be voiced. Maybe Kalli needed to hear from her mother's lips that her father, no matter how great he might have been, was not without flaws. If Kalli continued to carry around such an impossible mental picture of what a man should be, she would never commit to a relationship. No man could compete with such unattainable standards. Meeting a man and getting to know him would only heighten the problem. The first instant he showed a flaw, he would be dumped as surely as she'd dumped him on their aborted wedding day. Maybe he should consider himself lucky—to be dumped before his heart had become involved.

He flinched. There was something wrong with the way he'd put that. Shouldn't it have been before his heart could become involved?

Dion stood up and slapped Landon on the back, drawing Niko out of his musings. "Well, well," the old Greek bellowed, "I'm glad to see our worthy Zoe has found happiness, after years of being alone, raising her daughter and caring for her father-in-law." He pounded the table, making the silver and crystal dance and tinkle. "She deserves great happiness. This is a great, great day."

"Well, hell's bells!" Reece came out of his chair. "I never thought I'd live to see this, Landon, you old horse thief!" He tipped an imaginary hat and turned toward Kalli. "Sugar-darlin', we can't let these folks outshine us!" When he grasped her hand, Niko's gut clenched and he had the feeling the other big shoe was about to crash down with an explosion that would be hard to take.

Reece drew Kalli to her feet. "I'm a man of few words, little missy." He clutched her hands, his eyes aflame with purpose.

Though Niko could only see Kalli's profile, he watched her face. She looked confused.

"The first minute I clamped eyes on you I thought you were as pretty as a long-legged filly in a flower bed. I knew even then this moment would come."

Foreboding shot its cold, steel-toed boot to Niko's midsection. He flicked his blond friend a frosty look.

"Kalli?" Reece dropped to one knee. "I've been around the world and I've known a lot of women. But, by heaven, pretty lady, you've got me cinched up to the tightest hole, and I'm ready to pitch my little black book—if you'll agree to be my bride."

Kalli's soft gasp was the only sound in the vast room. Niko's attention was riveted on her face, what he could see of it. As her lips parted in either shock or awe, he mentally threw out reasons why she shouldn't accept, and he had no idea why. Reece was his best friend. He felt like a bum, hoping her answer would be no. What business was it of his from whom

she accepted or didn't accept marriage proposals? Maybe once it had been his business—a
month ago—but no longer.

She went pale for a short time, but quickly
her face flushed with a bright rosy color.

Reece grinned, ever the optimist. Niko was
furious with himself for caring one way or the
other. *Damn it, Reece is your oldest, closest
friend! Wish him luck, you miserable jerk!*

For a second, Kalli's lips moved but no
sound came. Her gaze skittered around the
room as she scanned the expectant faces.
When her glance met Niko's, he disguised his
anger and frustration with a facade of casual
curiosity. Her eyes were big and round, shimmering with reflected light. For a heartbeat her
regard seemed to sharpen, but the impression
was fleeting. In the next instant her attention
settled on Reece. ''I—I...''

''That had better be the beginning of I love
you, cowboy, and the answer's yes,'' Reece
coaxed. ''I'm letting it all hang out here,
sugar.''

Kalli felt disoriented, in a state of shock.
She bit her lower lip and blinked once, twice,
three times, only able to see Niko's face in her

mind's eye. When she'd chanced a peek at him, his expression couldn't have been more depressingly casual. His silent declaration of indifference cut deep, sending her tattered and confused emotions into a tailspin. She could hardly think, didn't want to. She looked at Reece, so handsome and strong, his expression both anxious and vulnerable. Her damaged heart went out to him; she couldn't humiliate him in front of everyone. It was too unkind. There was time enough to let him down easily—in private.

With an infinitesimal nod, she whispered, "Yes." She heard it, but in a fuzzy, mental haze. That one word sounded far away and seemed to have been uttered in somebody else's voice—one she didn't recognize. She felt disoriented, out-of-place, as though someone had dragged her kicking and screaming into the leading role of a surreal melodrama. She was soul-weary, on the verge of tears, so she'd opted to go with the flow. Saying yes was the path of least resistance. That decision was cowardly, and Kalli was appalled with herself for her lapse. Already, she regretted her decision to take the easy way out.

*   *   *

To Niko, Kalli's yes had the effect of a raw winter wind, moaning across an empty landscape, freezing his soul. He sat there smiling, censoring a pain in his heart he refused to acknowledge.

Reece leaped to his feet and let out a whoop, swinging Kalli in his arms. The other guests joined in the fun, laughing and cheering. Kalli's mother and Landon rushed to congratulate the couple. Zoe embraced her daughter and Landon clasped Reece in a bear hug.

Dion clapped his hands, though Niko caught a brief, accusing look out of the corner of his eyes that spoke volumes. The old man was saying, *See what your pride has cost you, Pal? Now, she is promised to another!*

Niko was in no mood to be chastised by his grandfather. Pushing up from his place, he strode around the table and did his duty to his friend. Extending a hand he said, ''Congratulations, Reece.'' His glance drifted on its own to Kalli, who looked painfully lovely with her peachy blush and temptingly curved mouth.

Reece took Niko's extended hand and pumped, but even his friend's exuberance couldn't force Niko's attention from Kalli's face. With effort, he managed a good-natured grin. "When I said I knew you'd find what you wanted," he murmured, "I had no idea it would be this soon."

Kalli was so ashamed of herself she couldn't stand to look in the mirror. How could she have said yes to Reece, even to save his pride? She had no intention of marrying him. Her rash acceptance to his marriage offer was an irrational, foolish backlash to Niko's obvious disinterest.

She'd hardly slept, tossing and turning with self-loathing. Yet, even as exhausted as she was, she had her wits about her now, and she knew what had to be done. Her failure in moral strength had to be corrected, her gutless vow withdrawn. Niko's disinterest didn't change the fact that she was *not* in love with Reece. He was a fine man who deserved far more than her feelings for him could deliver. One day he would find the right woman, someone who adored him and who would accept his proposal for all the right reasons. He had too much going for him not to find happiness, and she wished him well.

This morning he and Landon were leaving, having extended their visit longer than they'd intended. Kalli needed to set the record straight. *Now.*

She caught up with Reece in the foyer and silently thanked heaven he was alone. "Reece," she called in a half-whisper.

He turned as she hurried down the stairs. His grin was painfully happy and she felt like a bum.

"Good morning, sugar-darlin'." He held out both arms as though he expected her to run into them.

Instead she took his hands and pulled him out of the middle of the foyer into a secluded corner beneath the stairs. "Good morning," she said, her nervousness making her breathless.

He swooped down for a kiss, but she avoided it. "Wait, Reece," she said. "I have to tell you something."

He hesitated, his grin intact, though she noted a wary narrowing of his eyes.

She watched him closely for a second. "You know what I'm going to say, don't you?"

His smile dimmed a bit. "Haven't got a clue, sugar."

Her lips tipped upward in a melancholy smile. "I think you do." She squeezed his fingers. "Reece, about last night..."

His blond eyebrows came down, though he continued to grin. "What about it?"

She swallowed hard. "I—I feel terrible about this. But—when I said yes, I—I guess I got caught up in all the excitement." Wanting to let him down as easily as possible, she added, "I was flattered by your proposal. You're a marvelous man...so, well, I..." She shook her head, trying to find the words.

"Hell," he muttered, pulling from her grip. His hands lifted to clutch her upper arms. "Hell, sugar," he repeated, his expression bleak. "You're backing out? Turning me down?"

She bit her lower lip and nodded. "I'm so sorry. I—I guess I thought saying no last night would be too embarrassing for you." She realized she was looking him in the chest and made herself focus on his face. "Please—can you ever forgive me?"

His smile had finally died and there was a watchful fixity in his expression. After a tense moment, his lips lifted, but the smirk was brittle and lacked sincerity. "I guess I can forgive you, Kalli," he said, his long, slow drawl all but gone. "I'll take it like a man." He squeezed her arms, then let her go. "If Nik could deal with the humiliation of being dumped before all of San Francisco, I suppose I have the grit to survive being dumped this way."

His awkward smile softened slightly. "Be careful, darlin'," he cautioned. The Texas drawl was back. "You keep dumpin' men, and you'll get a reputation for being a mite fickle."

Kalli sensed Reece would heal, probably faster than her distress over this latest proposal mess would fade.

As she contemplated that, she felt a light kiss brush her forehead. "Have a good life, Kalli," he said. "I hope you never regret what you're doing—since I only ask once."

She flinched at his parting jab, but she couldn't blame him. She'd pricked his pride. "I'm so sorry," she murmured.

Dropping her gaze she stared at her hands, listening to the clomp of his boots as he walked out of her life.

Deciding her presence at the breakfast table would be uncomfortable for them both, she pivoted away and hurried up the steps. Halfway to the top, she came to a stumbling halt. Something Reece said belatedly sank in. *If Nik could deal with the humiliation of being dumped before all of San Francisco, I suppose I have the grit to survive being dumped this way.*

Before all of San Francisco? She froze, for the first time picturing what it must have been like for him—having to announce to a roomful of important people that his fiancée had just dumped—

She moaned and sank down to sit on a step. She'd been so deep in grief over her grandfather's death, she'd never even considered what her wedding day rejection would do to him. He'd told her she'd made him a laughingstock, but she'd never considered the extent of his humiliation. "It would have been in the newspaper and on the TV news," she mumbled, dropping her head to her hands. *Everybody would have known.* How did he stand it? "Niko, I'm so sorry. You must have been mortified! I'm surprised you didn't kill me!"

"Did you say something, madam?"

Kalli's head popped up at the butler's query. She had a sudden wild need to apologize to Niko for the great injury she'd caused him. She cleared the lump of emotion from her throat. "Uh—Belkin, has Niko gone in to breakfast yet?" She wanted to make amends, but not in public. If he were only still in his room.

"He had breakfast some time ago, miss."

Kalli looked at her watch. It was only seven o'clock. "That was early," she reflected aloud. Pushing up from the step, she faced the butler and brushed at the seat of her jeans, more out of nervousness than a concern for dust. "I—I need to speak with him. Where is he?"

"Gone, miss," Belkin said.

"Oh?" Kalli's nape tingled, and she rubbed it. Why was she getting a bad feeling? "When will he be back?"

"He won't be back, miss." The butler made the pronouncement so matter-of-factly it was hard for Kalli to absorb the magnitude of those ugly words.

"He—he won't?"

"No, miss," Belkin said with a benign smile, apparently unaware he was tearing out Kalli's heart. "Mr. Nikolos asked that I make his regrets to his guests, and explain that he had to fly to Zurich on urgent business."

The ponderous silence that followed seemed in danger of becoming permanent. Kalli grasped the stair rail and stared, disbelieving. She was so confused and miserable she couldn't even form a thought. What did he mean, Niko won't be coming back? "Won't?" she asked, needing clarification. "As in—never?"

"I would say so, miss. His penthouse apartment will be ready when he returns, and I've been instructed to close the house in preparation for the renovation, once your work is done."

Kalli hesitated, baffled, her brain barricading itself against the truth.

If Niko wasn't coming back—then she wouldn't see him again.

She winced, refusing to accept it.

"Will there be anything else, miss?"

Pulled from her musings, Kalli sucked in a quivery breath and shook her head. ''No—no, thank you, Belkin. Nothing.''

The servant disappeared without a sound, or did it only seem that way because Kalli's senses were completely focused on one bitter fact.

Niko was gone.

CHAPTER ELEVEN

KALLI trudged down the steps in an troubled stupor. Niko was gone. She drifted to the front door and went out into a chilly fog that seemed unusually bleak and gray and depressing. She walked down one step, dropped to sit on the porch and stared into the oppressive leaden soup.

Niko was gone.

"He's never coming back," she told the fog, hugging herself to ward off the chill. She was cold, colder than the brisk morning air would justify. Empty and sick at heart, she shuddered violently. Ice spread through her veins and brutal grief consumed her. Niko had walked out of her life without a "nice to have met you" or even a backward glance.

Feeling alone and cast aside, she stared into the nothingness, trying to fathom the reason she felt so miserable. In the past month she had rejected marriage proposals from two fine men, yet ironically, *she* felt discarded.

Because Niko was gone.

She dragged her hands through her hair and glared up at the shrouded sky. "Don't be in love with him, Kalli," she whispered brokenly. "Don't be that big a fool."

In less than a week, Kalli finished her work. When she and her mother returned to Kansas, her heart was little more than a deadened, broken ruin. Over the next several months as the restoration was being done, she made periodic trips to Niko's mansion. She loved the wonderful old place and each time she went back she fell more and more in love, as its unique beauty was slowly and painstakingly reborn.

She never saw Niko, but she constantly blessed him for allowing her the privilege of doing the restoration. *Architectural Digest* had already sent a cameraman and writer out to chronicle the mansion's recovery for a pictorial article. Without question, her reputation would be made; the sky would be the limit for her career.

Yet her heart couldn't be filled, refused to be light and gay. Even as her mother's wedding to Landon came and went, Kalli experienced only rare flickers of gladness. She had come to terms with Landon's new, cherished place in Zoe's heart, and wanted only the best for her mother. Landon was a fine person, as fine as her father, or so Zoe kept saying.

Kalli had never known her father to be hot-tempered or untidy or neglectful about saving for the future. Until recently, Zoe had protected Kalli from her daddy's failings, never revealing how far in debt they were when he died. Landon had none of the late Stefan Angelis's shortcomings, according to Zoe. Her new husband wasn't perfect, or expected to be, but he was a thoughtful, caring man who was good for Zoe and made her happy. Kalli was grateful her mother had once again found love.

In October, on her final trip to the mansion to check on last-minute details, Kalli chanced to look out a window and spotted Dion strolling through the field toward the house. She experienced a wild flutter in her chest and dashed outside, praying Niko had accompanied his grandfather.

"Dion!" she called, running through the formal gardens. She had no time for propriety or pretended nonchalance. She missed Niko.

She missed him with her whole heart and soul. No matter how long and hard she'd tried, she couldn't erase him from her thoughts. She loved him—the man she rejected on their wedding day. She loved him desperately and without hope. If Niko still harbored any desire for retribution, he had certainly won it, for she suffered night and day.

"Why, hello!" Dion called, with a friendly wave. "How nice to see you!" Natty as ever, in a dark suit and crisp white shirt, he held out both hands.

Her heart pounding unmercifully, Kalli grasped his blunt fingers. Was Niko near? Could he see her? Did she look a sight? She'd been so excited, she'd rushed outside without thinking to check her hair or her lipstick.

"It's great to see you, too, Dion," she said with a real smile. She hadn't realized how much she'd missed the old man, even though he's spent much of their relationship scolding her in his amiable, gentlemanly way. "You look fit and healthy," she added.

He laughed, a full-bodied sound that lifted her spirits. "And you are as beautiful as ever, dear child." He indicated the mansion. "I must say, you have done a wonderful thing. The house is perfection. Your mother must be proud of her accomplished daughter.''

Her cheeks grew hot with his compliments. ''I'm very pleased with the way the place has turned out.''

''Speaking of your mother, how is she?''

Dion had been to the August wedding, though Niko declined. Instead he'd invited Landon and his new bride to visit him in his penthouse upon returning from their honeymoon in Greece. They had visited Niko, though Zoe didn't comment on it beyond saying they'd seen him and he looked fine. Zoe clearly assumed Kalli's ex-fiancé was part of her past.

Sadly, that couldn't have been farther from the truth. Kalli recalled Niko's absence at her mother's wedding with great pain, a stinging, unspoken rejection of even the possibility of a friendship between them. She masked the pain with a smile. ''Mother and Landon are deliriously happy. They're building a lovely home on the Washington state coast.''

''Ah, that's fine, fine.''

"They've issued a blanket invitation for you to visit," she said. "How much longer will you be in the States?"

"Long enough to accept," he said with a hearty laugh.

"That's good. Then you'll be in California long enough to stay in Niko's mansion for a while, once it's completed. Which will be soon. I—I hope your grandson is happy living here." She wanted to ask, "Where is he? Did he drive out with you?" but she didn't dare, couldn't bring herself to, so she attempted to compel him to tell all by telepathically forcing an answer from his mind.

Dion's thick eyebrows knit. "I assumed you knew."

She had no idea why her comment would cause Dion's cheerful expression to vanish. "Knew what?"

"Niko won't be living here."

The revelation broadsided Kalli. She hadn't realized until that instant how much of her excitement to see the project completed was based on the fact that Niko would be the beneficiary of her hard work. Assuming he would live there, enjoying the fruits of her labor, gave her pleasure—and tiny bursts of hope. How many times had she daydreamed he would walk through the rooms she'd renovated and—possibly—think of her...maybe pick up the phone—

"Niko is donating the property to the American Cancer Society," Dion went on, cutting short her desperate fantasy. "Once restoration is complete, the home and grounds will be auctioned. All proceeds will go to charity."

"Oh..." She swallowed to ease a tightness in her throat. "I—no—I hadn't heard." She made every effort to look delighted. "A worthy cause. Some lucky family will get a—a fine home." She struggled to keep her voice from quivering. How foolish she'd been, dreaming Niko and she would one day share this marvelous manor, raise children there...

You rejected him, sneered the nasty troll in her head. *He's out of your life. You won't ever live here. You won't ever have Niko's babies! Forget it! Move on!*

She swiped at her cheek, hoping Dion would believe she whisked away a gnat rather than a tear. "Uh, why did he decide not to live here?" she asked, hoping she sounded casual.

"Since he bought the place as a wedding gift to you—" Dion shrugged "—he has no love for it."

Stunned by this news, Kalli could only stare.

Dion's expression grew concerned. "Are you ill, my dear?"

She shook her head to rattle her wits into place. "Me?" she squeaked. "Niko bought this place—for me?"

Dion seemed startled by her surprise. "Why, yes. Did he never tell you?"

She didn't think her spirits could sink lower, but this new revelation added a heavy, stinging layer to her seething guilt. "No—he never mentioned it." *Why didn't he? Wouldn't that knowledge—thinking this place might have been yours—have been perfect retribution for rejecting him on your wedding day? Why didn't he taunt you with the fact that he'd bought you this—this historic, magnificent...*

She cast an anguished glance over her shoulder to fill her eyes and her heart with the magnitude of Niko's gift. Tears welled and she blinked them back, getting herself under control before she faced Dion. "That was very generous of him," she murmured.

He nodded. "My Niko is a good boy."

No matter how destitute she was inside, Kalli couldn't help reacting to Dion's minimal evaluation of Niko's gift. The remark was so understated, she found herself giggling. The sound worried her, because she could detect a definite edge of hysteria. How could she feel both deeply touched and desperately sad at the same time?

Niko bought the house, not for himself, but for her. She'd loved the house before she realized she was in love with the man, and through her clumsy mishandling, she'd lost them both.

He has no love for it. Those few words echoed painfully in her mind, their ramifications making her go a little crazy. Her laughter grew helpless and shrill.

"Is anything wrong?" Dion asked, looking concerned.

"Wrong?" She waved off the question. "What could be wrong?" She gave him a brief, frantic hug. "I have to go." Spinning away, Kalli hurried off before her manic, bubbling glee became choking sobs.

*   *   *

In November autumn colors were in full riot in Kansas. Kalli wondered what California looked like. Was it cold and foggy or sunny and green? She could find out if she accepted the invitation that had just come in the mail. She supposed she shouldn't be surprised to be invited to the gala ball, when Niko's home would officially be donated to charity and auctioned off.

She stared at the shiny, gilded invitation, her heart arguing with her head. Niko would be there, of course. Did she dare go, dare risk seeing him? Since the gala included dancing, some tawny, reed-thin supermodel would be clinging to him. Could she cope with witnessing that?

''No,'' she said, rushing to the phone. She had to decline while she was perfectly lucid on the subject. She dialed the number listed for the RSVP, reciting over and over. ''I will not subject myself to Niko's indifference. I will not subject—hello?'' Some female on the other end responded with grating perkiness. Sticking to her resolve, Kalli refused the invitation and hung up the receiver.

She walked to the wastebasket beside her desk and disposed of the invitation. "I won't do it to myself," she muttered, taking her seat and thumbing through notes. She had two new clients to see this afternoon, both offering her exciting and profitable renovation projects. It was time she left Niko in the past where he clearly preferred to be. She had a burgeoning career on the horizon that needed care and feeding.

Wasn't there a song about how it never rained in California? Well, it lied, because it was raining tonight. Kalli dashed across the brick driveway, sorry she'd neglected to pack an umbrella. Though it was only sprinkling, by the time she entered Niko's mansion she would look like a wet dog.

"Fine," she groused as she sprinted, not easy in the beige crepe column dress and tapestry jacket she'd so painstakingly chosen. "What if he sees you, all water spotted, your hair plastered to your head?" She scurried toward the steps to the porch, angry with herself for this stupid, last-minute decision to come. "Just don't let him see you!" she muttered.

How the invitation had mysteriously removed itself from her wastebasket was anybody's guess. Surely she hadn't been so deranged she'd done it herself. However it happened, she rediscovered it this afternoon as it skulked between the pages of her day planner.

Somewhere between the time it arrived two weeks ago and the minute she unearthed it, her great bulwark of moral strength had eroded. A wayward gnome ruthlessly took over her body, and she found herself calling for flight schedules from Kansas City to San Francisco.

None of the remaining flights would get her there on time, but that didn't matter to the single-minded gnome manipulating her every move. She secured a plane ticket, snatched the dress she'd bought with such care—at the time of the purchase, she'd had no inkling why she'd taken such extreme pains—stuffed it into an overnight bag and dashed out of her apartment.

So, here she was at nine o'clock in the evening on a mid-November night running through the rain, somewhere outside San Francisco. She'd had to park her rented car way, way out in the boonies of Niko's estate. Sprinting up the front steps of the manor house she loved so well, Kalli found herself hoping for, yet dreading, a glimpse of Niko Varos. She was crazy. That was all there was to it—clinically and certifiably insane.

At the entrance, she swept damp hair out of her face and handed the guardian at the door her crumpled invitation. He waved her through with a smile. The manor was warm and welcoming and teeming with formally clad guests. The foyer sparkled with golden light from a huge, glittery and splendid chandelier. Equally splendid and exquisitely ornate, chandeliers in the nearby ballroom illuminated the large gathering of California's elite. All were there to celebrate this momentous occasion, many to bid on Kalli's masterpiece. That's what it was in her mind. A masterpiece. In her aching heart it was the home she would never share with the man she loved in vain.

Keeping to the shadows, she allowed her foolish need to lead her on. She had to see him, just once more. Then, she vowed, she would silently slip out and go back to Kansas. He would never know she'd come.

An orchestra played something soft and romantic as couples on the dance floor clung and swayed. Jewels of the megawealthy flashed and twinkled like flashbulbs. Laughter echoed off walls of rich burgundy William Morris woodblock wallpaper and plasterwork ceilings, restored and clean. She sucked in a breath of gratification to think she'd had a hand in returning the timeless beauty to this grand old dame.

A deep, familiar laugh echoed across the ballroom's din and her heart jumped a beat. She would never forget his laugh. Spinning in the direction of the sound, she instantly saw him—those compelling, smoky eyes, his mouth, firm and sensual, curved in an amiable grin. He towered above the crowd—tall, athletic; his elegant tuxedo fitted across powerful shoulders.

Unable to help herself, she crept close enough to hear as he chatted with guests. The timbre, the tone, the strong resonance of his voice, so reminiscent of their brief, tumultuous time together, brought tears to her eyes.

Kalli faced the fact she'd better escape before she made an idiot of herself. She fled out of the mansion into a heavy downpour. For once, she was thankful to be caught in the rain. None of the hired parking attendants in yellow slickers, carrying flashlights, would guess that some of the moisture on her face was salty, and hadn't fallen from the sky.

One pleasant young man guided her to her car, where it became frustratingly obvious a careless guest in a hurry had blocked any chance Kalli had of getting out. The attendant was sympathetic, and offered to have the owner of the offending vehicle paged. Kalli shook her head, assuring the man she was in no hurry and would wait in the rental until the car owner left. Her return flight wasn't until midmorning, and it was raining awfully hard. She didn't like driving during a cloudburst on dark, unfamiliar roads, especially in a strange car.

The attendant reluctantly left her as she slid into the driver's seat and waved him away with a brave smile. It only took minutes for her to realize she was too restless and overwrought to sit there and cry. She was weary of feeling sorry for herself. Angry that she couldn't seem to stiffen her backbone where Niko was concerned, she slammed out of the car. Rain or no rain, she needed to walk.

The weather was surprisingly warm. Or maybe she was just numb. She didn't care which. She only knew she needed to walk off her longing and frustration, so she headed across the lawn toward the field that lay between the manor and the cliffs.

Rain pelted her and her high heels sank into soft earth. After nearly turning her ankle, she kicked her ruined shoes into the dark. One of the parking attendants approached but she motioned him off with, ''I'm fine, thanks.''

After trudging some distance, she was finally far enough away so no more helpful young men bothered her. She glanced around. The mansion was off to her right and behind her. Golden light glowed from the arched windows, and even over the commotion of the shower, she thought she could hear the distant strains of dance music. Somewhere inside, in the light, the man she loved was dancing with another woman.

Listless and forlorn, she continued to walk aimlessly. After a while, she noticed the cliffs just ahead. She'd never come so close to the bluff before, and wondered why? On a clear day, the view must be spectacular. She recalled Niko's remark that she should look through a window from time to time instead of just at it. Her throat closed with regret for the many things she should have done differently.

Even in the pulverizing rain, she could hear the thunder of the surf. The powerful, profound bombardment resonated through her body, matched only by the unbearable clamor of her heartbeat. She wanted to scream out her sorrow and anguish for missing her chance at a love she discovered too late.

With leaden steps, she wandered haphazardly through the dark and rain. Though the night was black, her eyes adjusted. She stopped, squinting into the dimness. She thought she could make out a swing—a board hung between two sturdy lengths of rope and fastened to a high tree branch. A swing? It was an odd, out-of-the-way place, but she was grateful it was there. She hadn't realized how utterly drained she felt.

Weary and sick at heart, she dropped onto the wooden seat and stared out to sea. She imagined she could see the twinkle of light on the water. Perhaps a ship was sailing past in the darkness. More likely it was a trick of the night. What did it matter? She pushed off with her bare feet and swung, the motion oddly comforting. She lolled her head against the rope and swayed, kindred with the gloom and the rain.

She sat and swayed for a long time, wrapped in a cocoon of anguish. She became aware that the rain had eased, and gazed into the blackness above her. ''Grandpa Chris—'' Her voice cracked and she swallowed around the despair blocking her throat. ''Grandpa Chris,'' she repeated in a low moan, ''I'm the biggest fool on earth.''

Suddenly she was no longer swinging. A strong arm wrapped about her waist. Warm against her ear she heard, ''Don't go home with the crown, yet, Kalli. I've earned that title.''

Stunned, she turned to see Niko, his hair, his tux and his eyelashes dripping with rain. He moved to face her, taking off his jacket and gently placing it around her shoulders.

She could only stare, blinking in bafflement. He grasped the rope with both fists and slowly slid his hands down as he lowered himself to one knee. "You look wonderful," he said with a smile that seemed genuine.

Of course, it wasn't true and she couldn't believe him, but where was the teasing in his expression, his tone? Maybe it was too dark to see him clearly, and the pounding surf masked the scorn in his voice. "How—how did you know I was here?" she asked.

"Do you think you could walk into a room and I wouldn't know?"

She was confused, her wits apparently waterlogged to the point of being no good to her. What was he saying? Everything sounded like compliments—soft, gentle compliments.

She fought to get her mind on track. "Uh— donating the mansion was a commendable thing," she said, trying to be diplomatic. After all, it *was* a commendable thing—to everyone and in every way but in her own foolish daydreams. From the depths of her wounded soul she wanted to cry out, "I wish it was our home. I wish our children could run in the garden and play on this swing."

Slipping his hand over hers, clutching the rope, he asked, "What if I bought another one?'' The query drifted across the short distance between his lips and hers in a hushed whisper.

''I—I—that's—uh...'' His touch further short-circuited her brain. She could only stare and stammer, perplexed.

''If I did, would you make it perfect, too?''

Feeling disjointed, she said, ''Perfect?'' Hearing herself echo the word, she came partially out of her daze and struggled to get her brain working. ''Perfect—takes a long time,'' she said, needing to make light of the situation. He was teasing her and she must not allow it to defeat her. She didn't dare show him how much she was hurting.

''It would only take long enough for you to move in.''

She squinted, trying to make sense of this bizarre conversation.

He smiled the dearest smile. How unfair that she looked like something that had been washed up after a disaster at sea, while Niko seemed created to smile at a woman in the rain. The sight broke her heart.

''Will you marry me, Kalli?'' he whispered. ''Just one guy to one girl?''

She couldn't believe what she was hearing and she watched him warily. Did he know her composure was a fragile shell? Did he realize such blatant contempt would crack that shell and she would shatter in a million pieces? Was that what he was waiting to see? Had she really believed his desire for revenge had waned? How wrong could she have been?

"That's cruel," she whispered solemnly. "How dare you mock me like that." She swept wet hair out of her face and sat up straight, looking as poised as her battered emotions could contrive. "Please leave."

His smile disappeared. "I can't." He released her fingers only to take her face between his big, warm hands. "Not this time, Kalli. Not until you give me a straight yes or no to my proposal of marriage." His gaze was melancholy and soft as a caress. "As I said, I may win the crown as the world's biggest fool, but I have to tell you this or I'll never forgive myself."

His jaw clenched and his eyes narrowed slightly. "I fell in love with you when I saw your picture, Kalli. I guess that's why, when you rejected me, I was so—so angry. I didn't know it then, at least I tried to tell myself it wasn't true. But the more I tried to hate you, the more damned in love I fell.

''It hurt to know you didn't want me. And when you accepted Reece's proposal I couldn't stand it.'' His mouth twisted with self-deprecation. ''So, bloodied cur that I was, I crawled off to lick my wounds. I didn't know until Zoe and Landon came to visit that you'd broken your engagement to Reece.'' He leaned closer, whispering, ''I promised myself, if you came tonight, I wouldn't let you go without a fight.''

Her lips fell open, and she floundered before the brilliance of his eyes, the determination etched in his features. A warning voice whispered in her head, *Listen to the man before you do anything else stupid. I think he's serious. Don't blow it!*

When she tried to speak, she couldn't make any sound.

''Before you answer—'' he paused, his jaw muscles bunching ''—think about it long and hard, because if you accept this time, there's no backing out. I know there are no guarantees, but *blast it,* Kalli, if I can only love you when I want nothing more than to hate you, that's got to be a strong sign. If you care for me even a tenth of what I feel for you, we can make it.''

Her heart tripped and stumbled as she strove to decipher his meaning. Surely he couldn't be...it was impossible that he really...

When her mind finally allowed her to absorb the whole, unbelievable truth, her heart thrilled and soared. He was truly proposing marriage!

To her!

''Oh—oh, yes!'' she cried, breathless. ''*Yes, darling!* I'll marry you!''

He stilled, momentarily speechless as though he expected anything but a yes. An instant later, he recovered, his mouth curling with tenderness and relief. ''Thank the—'' He concluded his benediction against her lips.

Lifting her in his arms he took her place in the swing. Cradling her in his lap, he kissed her soundly, the masculine authority of his lips catapulting her to heaven. She luxuriated in his taste, his scent and his fire, full of promise for a sublime and lasting intimacy. In her woman's heart, Kalli knew his pledge to love and keep her was as everlasting as her own.

When they came up for air, she could hardly breathe, but she didn't care. She overflowed with a burning sweetness and uncontrollable joy. Niko was here, holding her like a lover, offering her forever. Her dreams were no longer hopeless fantasies. They were real.

How amazing that so much torment, grief and guilt could disappear in the face of one loving smile.

"Would you like to live here, darling?" he asked.

The question bewildered her. "What?"

"Because if you would, we still have time. The auction can't start until I get back."

"But—but Niko, didn't you donate the property to charity?"

He brushed her temple with a kiss, murmuring, "Yes, but I have as much right to bid as anyone."

An electric sparkle sizzled through her and she took in a quick breath of utter astonishment. "Do you mean it?"

"I want you to be happy, Kalli. Just say the word and I'll buy the place for you."

A great exaltation filled her to bursting. She didn't believe it was possible to be this happy.

The man she loved was willing to do such an extraordinary thing for her. "Again?" she whispered

He smiled, a lovely, wide warming smile that melted her to her core. "That's a yes?"

"Yes," she said, awestruck. His love for her was an endless surprise—endless, glorious and more dear to her than she could ever hope to define. "I love you so much, Niko," she cried softly. "I intend to prove it to you for the rest of my life."

"Ah," he said, teasing her lips with his own. "That's what I needed to hear." He lifted his gaze to the heavens. "Okay, okay, Grandpa—" his chuckle was husky with erotic promise "—give us nine months." He winked at Kalli. "Your grandpa wants—"

"Me, too, sweetheart." She pressed against him and slipped her arms about his middle. Kissing each corner of his mouth with provocative intent, she murmured, "The sooner the better."

EPILOGUE

THIS time there was no huge wedding or international guest list or formal attire, and most importantly, no renegade bride. This time, on a balmy, December day in sunny California, Nikolos Varos and Kalli Angelis were wed in an intimate ceremony in the formal gardens of their seaside estate.

This time there was no sadness to mar the blessed occasion, only smiles and well-wishes. Landon gave away his new daughter to his dear friend, Niko, as Zoe, matron of honor, cried tears of joy. Dion, as spiffy as ever, stood proudly by his grandson's side as best man. Even the weather was perfect and summery, the sun shining benevolently down to pay tribute to their union.

This time Kalli was indeed joined in holy matrimony to the man she loved. And to her utter amazement, she was actually going to live in the mansion she'd tenderly and affectionately refurbished.

Tugged from her happy musings, Kalli gasped as she was swept into strong arms.

"Where have you gone, my love?" Niko murmured near her ear.

She blinked, looking into gorgeous, smoky eyes, shimmering with a light Kalli recognized as the radiance of his love for her. She curled her arms around his neck and smiled contentedly. "I was thanking heaven for giving you to me."

His lips lifted in a gentle grin that stole her heart. "More like forced on you by the heavy-handed vengeance of a calculating bastard."

She shushed him, her expression both loving and admonishing. "I made a mistake by running away. You had every right to be angry."

He whisked her up the brick stairs toward their front door. "You were right to be doubtful. I treated you like a second-class client rather than a fiancée."

She kissed his cheek and giggled. "How did we get so lucky, after being so stupid?"

He halted at their front door, his gaze loving, even sweet. "I think that's where thanking heaven comes in." He glanced skyward for an instant then back at her. "And Grandpa Chris."

"Ah, yes." She drew forward and kissed his lips lightly, but with a sensual message her new status as his bride explicitly communicated. "Speaking of Grandpa Chris, sweetheart, if you'll recall, we have a promise to keep to him."

His grin grew roguish. "Exactly my thinking, darling." He turned the knob, allowing their front door to swing wide.

Kalli loved the sexy covenant in his eyes and laughed with giddy anticipation as the man she adored carried her across their threshold and nudged the door shut. The world outside would have to do without the newlyweds for a while.

Niko and Kalli Varos were very diligent, and promptly successful, in blending their two family trees. The following autumn brought with it the birth of bouncing baby Stefan Christos Dionysus Varos. A year later, beautiful Anastasia Zoe Varos would complete the family.

Needless to say, Grandpa Chris was very happy.

MILLS & BOON® PUBLISH EIGHT LARGE PRINT TITLES A MONTH. THESE ARE THE EIGHT TITLES FOR NOVEMBER 2001

❦

MISTRESS BY CONTRACT
Helen Bianchin

MARRIAGE AT HIS CONVENIENCE
Jacqueline Baird

A SPANISH AFFAIR
Helen Brooks

THE BOSS'S VIRGIN
Charlotte Lamb

HUSBANDS OF THE OUTBACK
Margaret Way & Barbara Hannay

THE MILLIONAIRE'S DAUGHTER
Sophie Weston

TO CATCH A BRIDE
Renee Roszel

HIS TROPHY WIFE
Leigh Michaels

MILLS & BOON®
Makes any time special™

MILLS & BOON® PUBLISH EIGHT LARGE PRINT TITLES A MONTH. THESE ARE THE EIGHT TITLES FOR DECEMBER 2001